ONE HUNDRED PROMISES

AN ASPEN COVE SMALL TOWN ROMANCE

KELLY COLLINS

CHAPTER ONE

Dr. Lydia Nichols stood on the sidewalk in front of the Aspen Cove Pharmacy. She prayed for lightning to strike from a cloudless sky, an avalanche to trigger from a snowless peak, a myocardial infarction to seize her healthy heart and end her miserable life.

Nothing arrived but a bee that sent her dashing down the street as fast as her clogs could take her. It was the only thing likely to grant her death wish. Making sense of her life was like trying to eat steak with a straw. How had it gone from gold to lead in such a short time?

Out of breath and back in front of the pharmacy, where the window sign flashed off and on with the red neon words The Doctor Is In, she stared at her reflection. The smiley face pin on her navy blue scrubs reminded her she had once been happy.

She pulled her shoulders back and prepared to leave purgatory and enter the fiery pits of hell.

Her mother had always said there were three certainties in life.

Death.

Taxes.

Change.

She'd dealt with her share of death, had paid enough taxes to pave the great state of Colorado, and was now dealing with change. A change destined to kill her hopes and dreams.

Lydia didn't see life's certainties in the same light as her mother had. There were three things and only three things she required to be happy. The first was a real job. The second was a man who gave more than he took. The third was an endless supply of coffee. A girl could really live if she had what she needed.

At thirty-two, she never expected to be in this position. Four years of college, four years of medical school, and a three-year residency had prepared her to be more than a country doctor—a fill-in at that. But a relationship gone bad with the head of emergency medicine at Denver General created change—change that came in the way of no job, no boyfriend, and no prospects for either. Maybe her mother had been right.

She was about to turn around and climb back into her car when the door opened and her sister rushed out of the pharmacy.

"You're here." Sage threw her arms around Lydia's neck and squeezed hard.

"I'm here," she said with the enthusiasm of someone getting a root canal.

"Why you wanted to show up midday and get straight to work, I have no idea. You should have taken a day or two to acclimate."

Her little sister had taken to Aspen Cove like a fish to water. Sage's life had come crashing down a year ago, but like the sun, she rose again. Lydia's lunar eclipse hadn't moved far enough to let even the tiniest fragments of light peek through her darkness.

"You know I'm not staying."

"But you're here for now, and that makes me happy. Doc Parker will be glad too."

She followed her sister into the small pharmacy. Calling it such was generous since it had nothing but over-the-counter meds or what the resident doctor finagled out of pharmaceutical representatives. Actual prescriptions were filled in Copper Creek.

"How's he doing?" A recent fire had compromised poor Doc's health. Although Lydia didn't believe in fate, she couldn't help but wonder if something larger was at work in the universe. Doc Parker's need for a temporary replacement had come at the time Lydia needed a job.

"He's still on oxygen, but his surly disposition is back so he's on the mend."

They weaved through the cold and flu aisle toward a door that led to the one and only examination room in the small clinic.

Folding chairs lined the wall. Three out of eight of them contained waiting patients. Having visited her sister the month prior, she recognized the first in line as Louise Williams, who was pregnant with her eighth child.

Lydia nodded as she passed and entered the exam room. The antiseptic smell was comforting, or at least it was familiar.

"It's a busier day than usual. Word got out you were coming to town, the books filled up for both clinic days. People are happy because they don't have to drive the hour to Copper Creek."

Lydia peeked out the door. "This is busy?" Accustomed to a big city emergency room where no less than a dozen patients waited, a handful of patients was nothing. In Denver, people were seen by the severity of their needs as opposed to a blocked set of minutes. Payment came in dollars, not firewood and casseroles.

"It's busy for Aspen Cove. The only busier day I remember was when the Williamses were here for vaccinations."

Lydia checked her pocket for a pen. She unrolled her stethoscope and hung it around her neck, then pasted on a smile as fake as her yellow pin.

"Shall we begin?" She looked around the small room and wished she could reach the two hundred miles to Denver and choke Dr. Adam McKay. This situation was his fault.

She glanced over Louise's chart while Sage stepped out to get their first patient. Eight babies in nine years must be a record.

"Dr. Nichols." Louise rushed inside. "I'm so glad you could come to Aspen Cove. We could use some new blood here and a female to boot. We hit the lottery." She stepped on the footstool and situated herself on the exam table like a pro. Then again, she was a pro.

"I'm not staying. This is temporary." She hoped she didn't have to remind each patient she was a fill-in while Doc Parker recovered.

"That's what everyone says and then they stay." Louise looked at Sage. "Sage once said it was a dream of hers for you to work together. Looks like dreams come true."

While Lydia examined Louise, her internal mantra repeated *this isn't my dream, this isn't my dream, this isn't my dream*.

Fifteen minutes later, her second patient walked in. Not walked as much as shuffled. Lydia glanced at his chart. "Mr. Bradley, I'm Dr. Nichols. What brings you in today?"

"Tilden brought me in. Good lad. Good driver. Single. You single?" The old man took five minutes to go from the door to the chair. He stared at the examination table and shook his head. "Not climbing up there, that's like climbing a mountain." He plopped into the plastic chair in the corner. The metal legs creaked under the weight of his three-hundred-pound body. "I'll stick to the lowlands. What about Tilden?"

"While I appreciate the attempted hookup, I'm not looking for a man." Lydia tilted her head and gave Sage a what-the-hell look. She wasn't in the market for a relationship—at least for the duration of her stay in Aspen Cove. She was happily single. Not happily, but single. After Adam, she needed a break from men.

It would take one heck of an amazing man to earn her trust. Men were like Bluetooth. They connected to you when you were nearby, but searched for other devices when you were away.

Sage moved forward to take the old man's vitals. "Ray here is our resident flirt. He's sweet on the ladies and has been known to empty a flower garden if he likes you."

In soiled jeans and a flannel shirt, he was straight off a mountain man poster—a cross between a geriatric Brawny model and grizzly bear.

"I'll never hear the end of stealing Bea's flowers."

"No flowers necessary, Mr. Bradley." Lydia said. "What health problem brings you in today?" She reviewed his file. Mr. Bradley had the usual problems associated with obesity like high blood pressure and high cholesterol. His last checkup was six months ago, and it didn't look like much had changed.

"I fell asleep at seven o'clock last night." He threaded his fingers through his ZZ Top beard.

"Do you have any other complaints?"

Sage checked his pulse and prepared to take his blood pressure with a wrist cuff.

"Ain't that enough? I missed my show."

"Ray is a huge fan of *60 Minutes*," Sage said as she wrote Ray's vitals.

A huff of air separated his beard to show thin chapped lips. "I feel cheated because I only got about three minutes before I dozed off."

Lydia looked through his record for a history of fatigue but found nothing. "Says here tomorrow is your birthday. You'll be sixty-eight."

"Well hell, no wonder I was tired." Ray rocked back and forth, then pushed to his feet and shuffled to the door. "Thanks, Doc." He moved out and down the hallway to disappear into the pharmacy.

Lydia shook her head. "That didn't happen, did it?"

Sage laughed. "You'll get used to it. Ray needed attention. Few women his age live here in Aspen Cove. He had to check out the new doctor in town."

"Should I fear him?"

"Only if you wake up to find hundreds of flowers on your doorstep. It won't be Ray you have to worry about but the owner of the garden he plundered."

Sage wiped down the counters with disinfectant even though they hadn't been touched. She was a qualified nurse, but Lydia couldn't understand how working at a tiny clinic fulfilled her dreams. Then again, Sage had a sexy fiancé to ease the rough edges of small-town life.

Lydia wanted more. She wanted a prominent job in a large hospital, a hefty paycheck to ease the burden of student loans, and a man she could trust. Finding a unicorn would be easier than reaching her goals.

She marked Ray's file with a note and placed it in the out-box on the counter. "Who's next?" She went to the sink to wash her hands and get fresh gloves.

"That would be Bailey. She's got something stuck up her nose."

Weeks ago, Lydia had triaged car accident victims and removed bullets from gangbangers. Today she was reminding people of their birthdays, examining a woman who had delivered more babies than she had, and her next patient was a kid who most likely shoved a bean up her nose.

She opened several drawers before she found a pair of sterilized forceps.

Bailey Brown bounced into the office with her pigtails swinging from side to side and hopped up onto the exam table. Her mother stood next to her like a sentry.

Lydia leaned over so she was eye-to-eye with the little freckle-faced girl who had a heartwarming smile.

She saw lots of children in the emergency room. This wouldn't be her first foreign object removal from an unusual orifice. It never ceased to amaze her what people stuck into their bodies.

"Hi, Bailey. I'm Dr. Nichols. Can you tell me what you put up your nose?" According to Bailey's chart, she was four years old and a regular at the clinic.

She looked behind to her mother. "No."

"No, you can't, or, no, you won't?" Lydia asked.

She glanced back to her mother and reaffirmed her position. "No."

Sage passed Lydia the otoscope.

"Okay then." She showed the child the instrument. "I'm

going to use this flashlight to take a peek. Can you look up for me?"

There was a moment when Lydia thought Bailey would refuse. Arms crossed and a frown as large as a rainbow on her face, she didn't move at first. Seeing she was outnumbered three adults to one, the little girl tilted her head and released a sigh of resignation.

Lydia peeked inside the tiny upturned nose. "What's your favorite, Skittles or M&M's?"

"Skittles," she answered with exuberance. "I like to save the yellow ones for last."

As her last word finished, Lydia tweezed out a sticky yellow Skittle. She put it into her gloved hand and held it out for everyone to see.

"Bailey," her mom scolded, "I told you you'd had enough and to put them away for another time."

Lydia turned to Mrs. Brown. "She did." She stared back to Bailey. "These are better in your mouth than in your nose."

Bailey smiled, plucked the yellow Skittle from Lydia's hand then popped it inside her mouth. All jaws dropped open except for Bailey who happily chewed her treat.

When she swallowed, she opened her mouth like a hungry bird.

Sage patted her head. "No Life Savers today, sweetie. That's Dr. Parker's thing. I'm sure Dr. Nichols will come up with something all her own for your next visit."

The disappointment on Bailey's face was unmistakable. She'd just had her nose plucked, and all she got was what she'd stored inside. Lydia took the child's hand and drew a smiley face on the back. Bailey grinned.

Mrs. Brown sucked in a breath. "We don't write on our hands, Dr. Nichols, it's a bad habit to start."

Lydia wanted to throw back something about eating nose Skittles being worse, but she refrained. "My apologies," she responded. When Memorial Hospital called and said they wanted her on staff, sticky yellow candy would be the furthest thing from her mind.

Going through three rounds of interviews had given her hope that an employment offer was forthcoming. Hell, she might be out of here before the ink faded from Bailey Brown's hand.

Sage showed them out while Lydia took a visual inventory of the clinic. It was well stocked with simple things for common occurrences like colds, cuts, and bruises. Standard equipment like oxygen tanks, IV supplies, and a sterilizer were present.

Nowhere did she see anything modern like an X-ray machine, electronic monitors, or an ultrasound.

Sage returned, pulled the paper off the table, and prepped it for the next patient.

"How can you work here?" Lydia turned in a circle and took in the lack of everything.

"What do you mean? It's great. When was the last time you got to know the people you treated? At Denver General, people are a number on a chart."

"This is like working out of a field tent. I didn't sign up for Doctors Without Borders."

Lydia found herself in a classic Sage Nichols hug. One she had to bear until it was over because Sage had a Super Glue grip.

"It's different. Not bad. We get cool cases like when Zachariah Tucker's moonshine still blew up."

Lydia let out a groan. "I never imagined my life being like this. I'm not moonshine. I'm a martini girl. I was headed for great things."

Sage stepped back. "You're still headed for great things, and Cannon can make a killer lemon drop martini." She rolled out fresh paper to cover the table. "Remember when Mom said there were three things you couldn't escape?"

"Death, taxes, and change. I remember."

"This is change, and change isn't always bad. A year ago you told me to come here and see what Aspen Cove offered. In fact, you likened me to Matthew McConaughey in *Failure to Launch*. You were right. I launched here in this small town, and I found my bliss. Maybe you should give it a chance."

In the distance, the bell above the door rang and Sage went to investigate.

She was back in seconds leading a man inside the examination room. He cradled his bloody right hand to his chest. His blood-soaked gray T-shirt stuck to his skin, outlining muscles forged from steel. More patients like this and Lydia would have to reconsider her man ban.

CHAPTER TWO

Wes Covington would rather be anywhere than a doctor's office. Looking at the gaping wound on his palm made his stomach turn and head spin. He pressed his bloody hand to his chest to stanch the endless flow. The deep cut meant stitches were likely. Stitches meant needles. A trickle of fear wormed its way down his spine. Wes didn't do needles.

"Geez, Wes, what the hell happened?" Sage moved like lightning around the room, gathering supplies while a sexy blonde in blue scrubs approached. She placed a comforting hand on his shoulder.

"I'm Dr. Nichols. I'm going to wash my hands and look at your injury. Can you tell me what happened?" Her voice was soft and sweet and soothing.

"I cut myself."

As a distraction, he stared at the doctor's backside while she scrubbed her hands no less than three times. It was a wonder she had any skin left when she snapped on a pair of gloves and approached him.

With tenderness, she took his hand in hers. "I'll need saline and sutures," she told Sage.

Sage prepped a tray with supplies that Wes didn't dare look at for fear of dropping like a stone to the linoleum floor.

"Can you glue it shut? Isn't that possible for some injuries?" He risked a glance at the tray, where Sage had readied a needle and thread. His head spun while his heart raced. The whoosh of blood pulsed through his ears, and spots of white danced before his eyes. A long deep breath pushed the dizziness away. With his uninjured hand, he gripped the table until his knuckles turned white.

Dr. Nichols's brow furrowed as she cleaned the cut. "I've got good news and bad news."

While she considered the injury, Wes assessed her. Long blond hair pulled into a ponytail. Blue-gray eyes the color of wet cement. Skin as smooth as his new granite kitchen counter. She was beautiful. Maybe this wouldn't be so bad.

That thought evaporated when he saw a smiley face pinned over her left breast. It was a reminder that this situation was anything but happy.

"Glue won't work here." She probed the cut, which no longer bled. "Too deep to glue. This needs sutures."

"Are you sure? It's stopped bleeding." He looked at the open wound. *Yep, deep enough for stitches.* "Please tell me that's the bad news."

"What did you cut it on?" Sage asked.

"Metal flashing," he replied.

"When was your last tetanus booster?" Lydia asked.

"My what?" He knew what a booster was. It was a shot, and he didn't do shots. "No idea." He wanted to kick himself for not coming up with an erroneous date. Something that would satisfy her need to inoculate. Then again she had his medical record and could disprove his lie.

Dr. Nichols smiled and looked at Sage. "He'll need a tetanus shot too."

His expression tightened so much the pinched furrow between his brows ached. "No shot."

"Yes, shots."

Did she say shots? "Shots? As in plural?" What started as a small tremble turned into a full body earthquake. "Where's the good news?"

Sage pulled what looked like a dog's pee pad from the cupboard and placed it on a rolling table in front of him. She lifted his shaking hand and set it in the center.

"You have to have a tetanus shot," Dr. Nichols said. "And you'll want me to numb up the area before I close the wound. The good news is I'll have you fixed up in no time."

Wes panted like he was in labor. Short spurts of air puffed between his lips. Every ten seconds he took in a larger breath and started the cycle over again. "I hate shots."

"Seriously?" The doctor stood in front of him with the same look his mother gave him years ago when he'd had a dozen shots for their trip to Africa. Only then, he'd already fainted and come to. "A big strong man like you isn't afraid of a needle, are you?"

Yes, I am. He'd rather come face to face with an angry bear than a needle. There was no rhyme or reason for the fear, but it was there. One look at the sharp pointed end and he'd be gone.

"I'm not afraid," he lied. There was no way he would embarrass himself in front of her. "I'm not a fan."

"Most people aren't, but they're a necessary evil."

"Evil is right. You sure I need a shot?"

"Shots." She laughed. It was like sunshine on a cloudy day. "Are you sure you're not afraid?"

He ignored her tease and changed the subject. "Nichols, that sounds familiar."

Sage stepped in front of the prep tray, blocking his view. "This is Lydia, she's my sister."

Lydia moved from behind Sage with a needle and a bottle of clear liquid. It was the last thing Wes saw.

He opened his eyes to blinding fluorescent lighting and the smell of ammonia floating beneath his nose. He blinked several times to focus.

Blond.

Blur.

Blue.

Smile.

"There you are," a sweet voice murmured.

What the hell happened? His fogged brain cleared as Lydia came into view.

"You fainted."

"I don't faint." He knew he did, but he couldn't and wouldn't admit to weakness.

"Oh, that was a faint all right. An Oscar-worthy performance, I'd say. Thankfully, you were already sitting, or you'd be on the ground. You went down like your joints collapsed."

He sat there in silence. "Are you really teasing me about losing consciousness? Don't you have a creed that prohibits you from preying on the weakness of your patients?"

Lydia's shoulders shook with silent laughter. "The Hippocratic Oath stipulates 'do no harm,' but I don't think it applies to egos."

"We're not talking about my ego here." Wes refused to look at his hand, which ached less than it did moments ago.

"Okay, Mr. I'm Not Afraid of Shots and I Don't Faint. You're ready to go."

His head snapped back. "Aren't you going to stitch me up?" Surely hitting the ground didn't nullify his requirement for care. He needed his hand mended so he could go back to work.

She gave him the same soul-scorching smile she had earlier. "More good news. It's already done. I followed my oath to do no harm. Since you aren't a fan of needles, I gave you the shot and sutured your wound while you took a little nap." The exaggerated wink she gave him said it all. She thought he was a wimp.

Sage handed him a bag with extra bandages. "If you come down with a fever or the area becomes red and inflamed, call us or come back in."

"You can take an over-the-counter pain med as needed for discomfort," Lydia added.

He looked between the sisters. They were as different as the sun and the moon. Sage had curly red hair, green eyes, and was the size of a leprechaun, while her sister resembled Malibu Barbie.

He walked into the pharmacy just as Doc Parker pushed through the front door carrying a small oxygen tank to his chest the way a mother might carry a baby. Behind Doc was Aunt Agatha who had become Doc's everything since the fire. It was nice to see the two had found happiness at their age.

"Wes, what did you do?" She rushed to him like the mother hen she was. Out of all his aunts and uncles, she was his favorite. Could be because she was the first to sell him her share of their historical family home called Guild House, but also because she had a heart dipped in gold.

He waved her off with his injured hand. "Just a cut, nothing to fuss over." He turned to Lydia with a pleading look and hoped she didn't embarrass him. To her credit she said nothing.

"What do I owe you?" Wes asked Doc as he followed him to the counter.

Doc shook his head. "No charge. You can come and give me some ideas on a remodel when you're healed."

"No charge?" Lydia asked. "How do you live if you charge nothing? How will I live?"

Doc Parker weaved his arm through hers and walked her toward the exam room. The last thing Wes heard before the door closed was Doc saying, "Money isn't everything. In Aspen Cove, we take care of our own."

Wes said goodbye to Sage and kissed his aunt on the cheek. With his ego hurting worse than his hand, and the orange glow of the sun setting between the buildings, he had two choices. He could go back to the house and wallow in his misery, or he could drown his embarrassment in a pint of beer. Beer sounded better. He stopped at his truck to change into the spare shirt he kept tucked behind the seat. He couldn't walk into Bishop's Brewhouse looking like he'd murdered someone.

When Wes entered, he found Cannon behind the bar with a notepad in his hand. Mike the one-eyed cat and full-time bar mouser sat on the cash register swishing his orange tail back and forth.

Cannon's eyes went straight to Wes's bandaged hand. "What the hell happened to you?"

"Got into a fight with some flashing and I lost, but your wife and her sister fixed me up."

"Not my wife yet. I got the ring on her finger, but I haven't been able to get her to commit to a date."

Cannon poured Wes a pint of stout. That was the beauty of small town living. Cannon knew his order without asking. When he went to the diner, Dalton knew he'd take the blue plate special. The bakery owner, Katie, made chocolate chip muffins with extra chips every Wednesday just for him. Life in a small town was simple. Wes liked simple.

"What's the story with her sister?"

"Lydia?" Cannon slid the mug across the scarred wooden surface. "Not really certain. She finished her residency at Denver General but hasn't found a job. There's something about an old boyfriend, but she's tightlipped about it."

Wes sipped at his beer. The light carbonation tickled. "They look nothing alike."

"Nope. My Sage is prettier."

Wes chuckled. He'd spent most of his summers in Aspen Cove until last year when he made the small town his permanent home. He would have bet that Cannon, Bowie, Dalton and he would remain bachelors forever. That all changed when they coupled up with Sage, Katie and Samantha. Nothing'd been the same since they came to Aspen Cove. Not worse or better for him, just different.

"The sister isn't hard on the eyes." He hadn't meant to say that out loud, but then again, nothing today went as planned.

"Are you interested? I've got connections."

Mike got bored with tail swishing and came over for a pet. He was an odd cat. Cannon had found him in a dumpster in the next town over. Mike was born with one eye. The cat loved to lap beer foam. Wes scooped some from his mug and put it on the counter for Mike to join him.

Another good thing about small town life was no one batted an eye at the feline patron.

"No, been there and done that."

"Is she still hounding you for money?" The *she* in question was his ex-wife, Courtney. They'd stayed married for three months. He saw her more now they were divorced than he did when they were married.

"I think I'll be paying for that mistake for the rest of my life."

"Just say no."

He took a long drink. Cannon was right. Their marriage was too short for her to claim anything substantial, but Wes provided the support she needed, regardless. It seemed the right thing to do.

Marrying Courtney was a great lesson in how to not choose a wife. They'd got caught up in each other and the sex. Mostly the sex. He never heard her say she wanted more—that she wanted a career in law and a life in the city. She never heard him say he wanted less—that living in Aspen Cove was enough. They were a runaway train waiting for a sharp turn. That turn came when she got accepted to Harvard Law.

"How's the house coming along?" Cannon pulled a jar of bar snacks from a shelf, filled a bowl, and set it on the counter in front of Wes.

He looked at his bandaged hand. "It's slow and will be slower now with the injury. The Guild Creative Center construction starts soon." Wes was excited to see his mother's family name live on in both the Guild House and the new center that would attract artists from all over. "I have to put most of my men on that project. I won't have much help, so I need a new plan. I'd love to finish the outside work by the end of summer, but that's a pie-in-the-sky dream."

"You'll do it. There's no rush. You've got the rest of your life."

"I do, but I feel we're in for a big change." Wes

wondered if the influx of new blood due to growth and expansion in Aspen Cove would change the dynamics of the small town he loved.

"Change is unavoidable."

The bell above the door rang and in walked two people Wes didn't know. That wasn't unusual since tourist season began in May. Add in the new flood of residents flocking to Aspen Cove and it was hard to tell who was staying and who was going.

Cannon walked to the end of the bar where the two men sat while Wes's mind went back to the sexy blonde doctor filling in for Doc Parker. How long was she staying?

As if summoned by his thoughts, she walked into the bar with Sage and took the stool next to him.

CHAPTER THREE

Lydia swatted Mike from the bar top and asked her sister for disinfectant. Since Sage was engaged to the owner it wasn't a problem for her to walk behind the counter.

"I can't even think about how unsanitary this counter is," Lydia commented.

"Then don't," Wes said. "Can I get you a beer? Since I couldn't pay for your services, the least I can offer is to pay for a drink."

She rolled her eyes. "I'll never understand how places like this work." Sage set a spray bottle and a terry cloth in front of her. Lydia handed Wes his beer and sprayed his area too. "How is someone supposed to succeed in life if they're paid in favors and cheesy casseroles? I'd starve to death."

He shook his head. "No, you wouldn't, you can survive on dairy and noodles."

A long sigh emptied her lungs. "I want more." She turned to Wes, who nursed a beer.

"Everyone wants something different."

Cannon stopped in front of her. "Lager or wine?"

"I'll take the beer."

"See, if you were a regular, he wouldn't have to ask. He would have had it waiting here at the exact time you were expected to show up."

"Who wants that? What if I changed my mind?" She hadn't changed her mind about him. He was still as sexy as he'd been an hour ago. Maybe sexier, since his skin had color and was missing the sheen of fear-induced sweat. She took in his chiseled jaw, sensual lips, strong nose, and seductive eyes. She hadn't noticed before, but they were brown with specks of amber that reminded her of the topaz ring she inherited when her mother passed away.

"Do you do that often?"

Lost in his eyes, she'd forgotten the conversation. "Do what often?"

"Change your mind?"

She thought about the question for a moment. "Nope. I'm solid with my wants and desires."

He turned toward her and picked up his half-empty mug with his injured hand. A look of pain shot across his face and the mug dropped to the surface without a spill. "Right handed." He shrugged. "I'll have to get used to being ambidextrous."

"Big word for a country boy." She took in his half-empty beer. "You know when I said take over-the-counter pain meds, I didn't mean this kind of counter. A good anti-inflammatory would work better than beer."

He cocked his brow. "Anti what?" He lifted his beer to his lips with his good hand. "That's too big of a word for a simpleton like me."

She felt the heat of embarrassment color her cheeks. "That's not what I meant."

"Isn't it?"

He drained his mug and dug into his pocket for the five-dollar bill he tossed on the bar. He rose from his stool and waved to Cannon before he turned to her. "See ya round, Doc."

She glanced at the money he left. He'd pay for his beer but not for his care. That's why she knew her life in Aspen Cove would be short. Small towns had their priorities skewed.

Sage plopped onto the stool Wes had vacated. "He's cute, right?"

Lydia looked over her shoulder at his retreating figure. "If you like zeta males."

"Oh, please..." Sage argued. "Wes is far from zeta. Just because he doesn't like needles doesn't make him weak or less of a man."

"I'm not saying he's less of a man. Being a man gives him a blemish in my book. He may be an alpha with a capital A, but I'm into my Z game which means I have zip, zilch, zero interest in any man." It was hard not to roll her eyes at herself. She was interested but afraid to take another leap for fear of free-falling off a cliff.

"You can't blame the male species for Adam's lack of integrity." Sage sipped the glass of wine Cannon placed in front of her.

Lydia knew she couldn't harbor resentment against all men, but until something in her life turned around, she'd treat them like bees. Better to avoid them altogether than take the risk of getting stung.

"Adam was an asshole." Each time she heard his name, her gut twisted and acid rose up to burn her throat. "He treated me like an old worn shoe and tossed me in the corner when he was done."

"Grandma Dotty always said it takes two to tango. You

guys didn't get to the place where it ended alone. Until you figure out your part, you're destined to repeat it. As for shoes... you're not old and worn. You're like a pair of heels that look pretty but hurt like hell to wear long-term."

Lydia's jaw dropped open. "Thanks for the advice, Dear Abby, but I didn't do anything to make Adam cheat on me with that oncology nurse."

Sage twisted in her seat. The position had them sitting knee-to-knee, eye-to-eye. "What bothers you more, that he cheated at all, or he cheated with a nurse when he had a doctor at home?"

Sage knew exactly what buttons to push to drive Lydia over the edge. "Isn't cheating enough?" What did it matter if she was a nurse or she was prettier and younger? "That man lived free and clear at my house for years. I did everything for him from make the staff schedule to wash his clothes, and he still left me. You know what really chars my ass? He bought a house with all the money he saved free-loading on me and moved her into it." She picked up her mug, emptied it, and slid it down the bar toward Cannon, who was chatting with the two men at the end. "Refill please," she asked when he glanced her way. In seconds, she had another cold one in front of her. It might take a dozen to ice the heat burning inside her.

"You created that situation." Sage leaned on the bar. "All I hear you saying is everything you did for him. What did you do for yourself?"

That was an interesting question Lydia hadn't considered. "I earned my degree and became a doctor."

"Was it worth it?"

"Him cheating on me and being a doctor are unrelated." She drew several smiley faces in the frost of her mug before she palmed the glass so they'd disappear.

"Are they?" Sage laid her hand on Lydia's arm. It was a warm gesture that spoke of her love for her sister. "Why did you give yourself the night shift when Adam worked days? Why did you allow him to be a taker instead of demanding he give? You treated him like you treated me. Like somehow it was your responsibility to take care of him. Did you ever consider that he wasn't looking for a mother but a partner?"

Lydia stared at her beer and watched the bubbles burst. Sage's words, though not meant to be harsh, cut like a dull, rusty blade. She wanted to lash out and say Adam wouldn't sleep with his mother. Then again, he'd stopped sleeping with her long before he moved out. As painful as the words were, they were truthful.

"I get what you're saying, but I tried to be who I thought you needed. Who he needed."

Sage leaned forward so their noses almost touched. "That was your biggest mistake. You needed to be you. While you were helping everyone find themselves, you lost you."

When was the last time Lydia had been herself? Everything changed when her parents died. At sixteen, she'd grown up overnight. Instead of worrying about first dates and prom dresses, she fretted over her sister and her grandmother. She redirected her angst to make sure they were nurtured and looked after.

"I don't know who I am anymore." A single tear slipped down her cheek.

"Maybe you should take the time to find out." Sage's kiss to her cheek reminded her of their mother's compassionate and caring nature. It was almost as if her spirit sat at the bar with them.

Lydia looked at the clock on her phone. "I'm beat." She

slid her untouched beer to her sister. "You drink it. I'm going to head home and call it a night."

Sage leaned forward and gave her sister a hug. "Katie said the keys are under the mat."

"Yep." All Lydia wanted was a quiet place to think and a comfortable bed to sleep in. "I'll be okay."

"Yes. You will. Don't forget we have the ribbon cutting for the park on Saturday, but I'm sure I'll see you before then."

"That you will." It wasn't like Aspen Cove was a mecca for entertainment and options. Sad but true, the park opening would be the biggest event of the year.

When Lydia tried to leave money on the counter, Sage shook her head. "You're family. It's a perk."

"I can use a perk or two." She rose from her stool. "What's on the agenda tomorrow?"

"Not a thing. The clinic isn't open."

"Right." She wondered if increasing clinic hours would increase its profitability. Then again, Doc made a point that Aspen Cove took care of its own as he'd walked her back to the examination room and handed her a check for her first week. When she told him she worked before she got paid, he told her to take the check and stop complaining.

Lydia was certain he'd paid for her services in advance so she couldn't leave.

She drove her car to the alleyway behind the bakery and the bait and tackle shop and pulled her overnight bag from the rear seat of her car. She could come back for the rest later. At the back door of the bakery, she found the keys where Katie said they'd be, under the smiley face mat. Was that a coincidence or had Sage told her about her love of all things smiley?

She unlocked the door and trudged up the flight of

stairs. It wasn't her two-story house in the suburbs of Denver, but for now it was home. At the top she opened the next door and entered her new digs. On the coffee table was a large vase of sunflowers and a notecard from Bowie and Katie. She was grateful that her sister had made such good friends in town. Grateful they had accepted her as a friend so easily.

Welcome Home Doc,

There are staples in the refrigerator. This apartment comes with unlimited muffins and fresh brewed coffee.

So glad you're here in Aspen Cove.

Hugs,

Katie and Bowie

She set the card down and walked to the window that looked over the town. On the sill lay several dead bees. *Better you than me.*

CHAPTER FOUR

Wes parked in the driveway and stood in front of his house. *His house.* He never thought he'd see the day his aunts and uncles would come together and do the right thing. They'd been fighting over family assets since his great-grandfather Thomas passed away.

It was a good thing the papers were signed before the old paper mill was purchased, otherwise, he'd be living on Hyacinth Street in a smaller bungalow instead of Rose Lane in the big Victorian built by his ancestors. They would have never sold the property if they thought Aspen Cove could become the booming town it once was and with the plans to turn the old Guild Paper Mill into the Guild Creative Center, growth was a guarantee.

He was no sooner out of his truck and through the front door when Sarge barreled into him. The old German shepherd acted like a puppy even though he was nearing seventy in dog years.

"Hey, boy." Wes rubbed the top of his head and waited for Sarge to sniff out the goods. Being a retired narcotics canine officer, he had a well-trained nose. The dog circled him several times before he pressed his snout into Wes's ankle, the exact place he'd shoved a milk bone before he exited his truck.

"Good boy." All Wes had to do was expose his sock and Sarge retrieved his prize. They went their separate ways with the shepherd heading into the living room for a snack while Wes went to the kitchen for a late meal.

He rummaged around his refrigerator for leftover pizza. He couldn't remember when he bought it. Was it four days ago or a week ago? Once he flipped open the box and didn't see mold, it didn't matter. The great thing about pizza was it didn't have to be heated. He pulled a slice out and ate it while he made the rounds of the house. It was something he did each evening. With every walk-through he moved something from his to-do list to the done column. The only thing he accomplished today was to ruin a T-shirt and embarrass himself in front of Dr. Nichols. The jury was still out regarding the blonde with the big attitude. He wasn't sure if he liked her or not. She intrigued him for sure, but maybe that was because she was like a shiny new penny in town.

He fell onto the couch and stared at the old Van Briggle fireplace tiles. Blues and greens washed the surface. He always smiled when he thought of those tiles and the months he spent removing soot and grime to uncover the beauty beneath. Wasn't that the way of the world? His mind went to Lydia, who was pretty, but he could see the soot and buildup of a tough life covering her and wondered what she'd be like if someone spent the time to get to the beauty she held within.

A knock sounded at the door. Sarge wagged his tail and rushed to greet their guests. It had to be someone familiar because a stranger would have gotten a growl. When he opened the door, Samantha and Dalton stood in front of him.

"We had a meeting to go over the plans, didn't we?" Wes had forgotten. Had he hit his head when he fainted? "Come on in." He stepped aside and made room for his larger-than-life friend and his tiny girlfriend.

They stared down at Wes's bandaged hand. "We can reschedule," Samantha said.

He shook his head and waved them toward the dining room. It was the only room with a surface big enough to spread out the plans Dalton held in his hands. "No, it's great. I lost track of time. Come on back."

They followed him to the back of the house where an old Duncan Phyfe dining room table sat like a trophy in the center of the room. It had taken Wes a year of begging to get his mother to part with the antique. She let it go when he offered twice what it was worth and pointed out it didn't match the architecture of her modern loft. With the Covingtons, everything was a fight.

Dalton opened the building plans and rolled the edges so they lay flat. "We love almost everything."

Wes hated the word *almost*. *Almost* got you nowhere. It was a word he'd heard all his life. That's almost perfect. You're almost there. It was a kind word that meant you missed the mark.

"You want a beer?" When they both nodded, he grabbed three from his fabulous new refrigerator. The only thing that would make it better would be if it shopped for itself.

When he returned, Dalton and Samantha were huddled over the first page. Few people knew he was an award-winning architect. It wasn't something he bragged about because he'd rather build things than design them, but when Samantha bought the old mill that once belonged to his family, Wes felt like he had an obligation to make sure the building was handled in a way that respected the past while they moved the building into the future.

"Tell me what you don't like." He opened a china hutch drawer and grabbed a pen.

"Did we say we didn't like something?"

Wes chuckled. "You said it was almost perfect, which means something needs improvement."

The couple looked at each other and smiled. They proved that having less could be so much more. Samantha was a multimillionaire pop star and preferred to live in Dalton's two-bedroom cabin. She once told him she was rich in love, which was far better to collect than cash.

Dalton picked up the pencil from the table. "Sockets. I need more sockets." He drew in several more boxes along the kitchen walls and prep tables.

Wes was excited to see Dalton get his dream culinary school placed beside Samantha's new recording studio. When other creative people leased the remaining spaces, there was no doubt the town would grow.

"That's all? You want more sockets?" Wes expected a major reconfiguration, not a request for additional power receptacles. "I'll give you all the sockets you want."

"It's going to be amazing, isn't it?" Samantha bounced with enthusiasm.

"Yes. I'm so glad you saw the place for the goldmine it is." He'd played in the paper mill as a child. He might carry the last name Covington, but he was a Guild on his mother's side. Many people didn't believe in preserving the past, but for Wes there was a lot to learn from his ancestors. They worked an honest day for decent wages. Work and play were separate. One didn't bleed into the other. Cell phones didn't exist. The internet wasn't even a concept back then. Weekends were for the family. Stores didn't open on Christmas Day. Life was less complicated.

"It's perfect." Samantha left Dalton's side and threw her arms around Wes for a hug. "When can we get started?"

"Right away. When is your next album due?" That was the real determining factor. Samantha's recording studio would be the first thing built since she was financing the project. Wes loved that a place that created paper would become a place to create. He knew if his great-grandpa Thomas could see the old mill when it was done he'd be proud.

"I have to deliver by the end of the year, but the hardest part is finished. The songs are already written."

"Our biggest hurdle is getting enough people hired. I'm meeting with the Lockhart brothers tomorrow. They own a small construction business in Cross Creek. I'm hoping to subcontract them out for the duration. They have a stellar reputation. If it works out, we'll get started this week. Once the Guild Creative Center is built, we can move on to flipping houses. The people who rent the new spaces will want great places to live."

Dalton grabbed the end of the plans and rolled them into a tube. "How are the permits coming along for the firehouse?"

That's where the big problems began. Aspen Cove was a small town and didn't have a zoning commission, so permits came through Copper Creek whose mayor coined the word *nepotism*. His children filled all the important city positions. Craig Caswell ran the permits department like he was God building the universe. Only he didn't have a seven-day plan.

"I'm expecting to break ground in two weeks. Provided

everything goes as planned, the Aspen Cove Fire Department should be ready by September. I've secured a company from Denver. They built the station in Cherry Creek. Not only is it high quality, but also state-of-the-art."

Wes told no one he'd been the architect of that project. It was the last job he worked on before he left Covington Architecture and Design. He could still hear his father's voice telling him it was almost good enough. Funny how his tune changed when it came in under budget and won a coveted sustainability award.

"That's a relief." Samantha's manager had started a fire that had burned down her house and injured several townsfolk. No matter how many times people told Samantha the fire wasn't her fault, she continued to blame herself.

Her self-induced penance was to build Aspen Cove a firehouse, so no one had to depend on volunteers to save their lives.

"It's under control." He offered his hand to Dalton for a shake and pulled it back when he realized how painful that would have been. The man was as big as an oak tree and no doubt had a powerful grip.

"What happened to you?" Dalton wrapped his arm around Samantha and pulled her close.

Wes wondered if they even realized how many times they touched each other. A pang of jealousy threaded through him. He wanted what they had. He wanted a partner to share his life. He wanted a woman who valued love above everything else. "It's just a cut. I was working on a window sash and some metal flashing got the best of me."

"That means you met Lydia. Isn't she the best?" Samantha asked.

"The best what?" He led them to the front door.

"She's so smart and sweet." Samantha nearly burst with

enthusiasm. Wes wondered where she got her energy. He imagined Dalton and she fed off each other. He'd never seen two people so happy together.

"*Sweet* isn't the first word that comes to mind, but she stitched me up."

Wes closed the door and went back into the living room, where his dog had taken his place on the couch. He nudged the dog over and squeezed into the small spot Sarge allowed. "It's just you and me, buddy." Sarge looked at him with the same love Dalton had for Samantha and Wes wondered if he'd ever find that love and devotion with a woman.

CHAPTER FIVE

There was no way Lydia could live long term in a place where the walls buzzed as if alive. The sound never stopped for a second. She couldn't figure out if it was the hum of the heater, a motor gone bad in the refrigerator, or if the ovens had been left on downstairs. All she knew was it kept her awake all night long.

She trudged from the bedroom down the hallway to the bathroom. Dark circles painted her eyes and spoke to the sleep she hadn't gotten in weeks. After a quick shower, she threw on clean clothes, brushed her teeth and ran a brush through her tangled hair. Clean and presentable was all she could hope for today.

The sweet smell of muffins seeped through the floorboards. Her sister told her she could set her calendar by the muffin of the day. If her nose scented the lemon correctly, it was poppy-seed muffin day. Her mind might be tired, but her stomach was ready for food.

She flung her purse over her shoulder and walked into the dark living room, where she came to a dead stop. With a big picture window looking east, the room should have been bathed in morning light, but thousands of bees looking for an exit draped the glass like a curtain.

As Lydia's heart rate picked up so did the hum. She reached into her bag for her EpiPen and backed her way to the door. When several bees dive-bombed her head, she gave up slow movements and raced for the exit, slamming the door behind her. The whir of the bees increased as she ran down the steps and out the ground level door. She didn't slow down until she made it around the building and into the pharmacy. Once inside, she crouched by the window.

"You've only been here a day and you're hiding?" Doc's familiar voice said from behind.

"Bees." Out of breath, it was the only word she could vocalize.

"You're hiding from bees? You think they're hunting you down?" The hiss of his oxygen tank matched the cadence of his steps. "I don't think they're that smart. Instinctual for sure, but planners? Nope."

"There's no way I'm staying."

Doc crouched down beside Lydia. "I didn't take you for a quitter."

She shook her head to clear her thoughts and stared at the old man in front of her. "I'm not a quitter."

"Leaving here without giving it a chance is what I'd call quitting."

Lydia stood to her full height of five foot six and fisted her hips, still gripping the EpiPen. "Have you heard nothing? There are bees." She shoved the pen back into her purse and marched over to the candy rack and took an Abba-Zabba. At least it had peanut butter in it, which could be considered healthy protein.

Doc walked to where Lydia stood chewing on sweet nougat.

"Just like crime, bees have no address. You find them everywhere."

Lydia shook her head so hard her brain hurt. "They have an address all right. Thousands of them are living in my apartment."

It took Doc a minute to process the information. When his white brows lifted toward the ceiling, Lydia knew he understood.

"I'd say call Abby, but she's visiting her sister in California for a few weeks."

Lydia reached for another candy bar but Doc pulled it away. "I've got muffins upstairs. How about you and I have a cup of coffee and a muffin while we figure this out?"

She followed him up the back stairs to an apartment much like the one she was supposed to live in. The only difference was Doc's place smelled like Bengay and Old Spice and didn't buzz like a hive.

He led her into the small galley kitchen and pointed to the table in the corner. Within minutes, they were having breakfast and making plans.

"Can't I call an exterminator?"

By the gasp and wheeze from Doc she figured that was the wrong approach.

"What have those bees done to you to deserve extermination? In Aspen Cove we take care of our own and that includes our bees." Doc sipped his coffee. "I imagine those bees escaped the hives during the fire. Sure would be a shame to kill them off after they survived that mess."

Put that way, an inkling of guilt needled its way into Lydia's chest. She reached into her purse and pulled out her only defense against a bee sting. "It's me or the bees, and I'll choose me every time."

Doc's eyes grew wide. "How bad?"

"Severe anaphylaxis."

The last time she got stung had been a good ten years ago. All she remembered was sitting in the grass of the commons area at college. A bee landed on her leg. When she swatted it off, it stung her. Everything else happened so quickly. The sting blazed through her system like an out-of-control fire. Her skin burned and itched. The venom wrapped around her neck like a noose and squeezed and squeezed until she lost consciousness.

She woke up at Denver General in the ICU. It was the first time she met Adam McKay. He was the doctor on call. Right then she decided emergency medicine would be her specialty and Dr. McKay would be her man. How funny that sometimes you get what you ask for and it's not what you wanted at all.

"You can't stay there."

Lydia pulled the top off her muffin and slathered it with butter. "The first thing we've agreed on." She took a bite and hummed. Bees might send her running from Aspen Cove, but Katie's muffins made a good argument for staying.

Doc picked up his phone and dialed a number. After a moment he said, "Abby, sorry to bother you but thought you should know your bees are safe."

Lydia finished her breakfast while Doc Parker explained the situation. Abby offered her place to Lydia until she could get back to town to extricate the hive, but since Abby specialized in bees and honey, her land was surrounded by hives.

The next call was one Lydia made to her sister. Certainly a woman who ran a bed and breakfast would have a room at the inn for her sister, but as bad luck would have it, the place was booked solid until the end of summer. All she could offer was the couch. Lydia reached out to everyone she'd met on her last visit to Aspen Cove, but no one could offer her a place to stay.

Katie was mortified to find out the apartment was full of bees, but she didn't have a solution. She promised as soon as Abby got the bees cleared she'd have the apartment ready again. Samantha and Dalton were her last chance but their house was small with the spare room holding all of Samantha's things until they could move them into the studio. Lydia's bad situation turned worse with no place to go.

Footsteps on the stairs had them both watching the door when Doc's girlfriend Agatha walked inside his kitchen. She placed a paper bag on the table and bent over to give him a peck on the lips.

"Everything okay?" She went about putting away the groceries she picked up at Target. If the big red bull's-eye on the bag wasn't her first clue, the second was the fresh-looking produce. The Corner Store had nothing fresh.

"We're in a pickle here," Doc began. He described Lydia's housing dilemma, which was a problem for Doc Parker as well because if Lydia had nowhere to live, she couldn't stay and work in the clinic. It was hard to tell whether this new turn of events was more bad luck or a message from the universe telling her to cut and run.

"No pickle at all. I'll have you a room in a minute." Agatha dug through her purse to get her phone. She squinted at the screen and pressed it several times as if pushing the call button the first time wouldn't work.

Lydia noticed as people aged they got impatient. Maybe they were afraid the call wouldn't go through before they died. Pushing the button repeatedly didn't help, but since

Agatha seemed to have a solution to her homeless problem, Lydia kept her criticism to herself.

The echo of a distant ring filled the silent kitchen until a deep voice answered, "Hello."

"Sweetheart, this is Aunt Agatha. Can you spare a room for Doc's replacement? There seems to be a problem with her current lodging arrangements." Agatha pointed to the phone and whispered, "My nephew." There were a lot of uh-huhs and okays. "That's great. I'll send her right over."

Doc left the room while Agatha wrote an address and passed it to her. "Head on over, dear, he's waiting for you." She turned away and continued to talk to her nephew.

Lydia gathered her things and called out, "See you later, Doc," hoping he heard her.

She rounded the back of the building with trepidation, somehow expecting a swarm of bees around her car. To her relief, there was nothing.

She hopped inside and laid her head against the steering wheel. Grandma Dotty used to tell her that life slapped you upside the head when you weren't getting a clue. It started as a light tap and increased until the lessons came like hammers. Lydia figured she was at the sledgehammer stage, but what was the lesson she'd missed?

Her thoughts went back to last night at the bar and Sage's comment about her taking responsibility for her part in the breakup with Adam. If she was honest with herself, she'd created a gaping hole in their relationship when she volunteered for every class and took the bad shifts so others wouldn't have to. She thought she was doing the right thing, but all she had done was leave the window open for another woman to climb through.

She banged her head against the steering wheel several times before she started the car and drove to 10 Rose Lane.

Parked outside of a beautiful Victorian home she read the inscription above the door where gold letters etched The Guild House into the wood.

Turns out there were several founding families in Aspen Cove. Sage once told her the Guilds arrived first followed by the Bennetts and then the Parkers. Little by little a thriving community was born because the first person gave Aspen Cove a chance.

Lydia finger-combed her hair and pinched her cheeks pink. No sense in scaring off whoever lived here. She needed a place to live otherwise she'd be sleeping on her sister's couch or sharing a floor cushion in the corner with her three-legged dog Otis.

Drawing in a deep breath, she walked to the front door and raised her hand to knock when it flew open and none other than Wes Covington stood in the entry.

"You're the nephew?"

"Great nephew." He stood aside for her to enter. "I hear you need a room."

Lydia wanted to turn and run. Of course it would be Wes because karma was a spiteful bitch. With no other options, she stepped into the entry where the small space seemed to wrap around her like a comforting hug.

Someone with a keen eye had chosen a soft gray-blue that happily took a back seat to an ornately carved staircase. The beauty was in the details. While the staircase was nice, and the wall color the perfect choice, it was the simplicity of the hand-scraped wood floor that gave the space its warmth. The soft undulating texture promised to lead her to something more if she dared to walk down it.

"This is yours?"

He led her down the hallway to a beautiful but messy

kitchen. Once again, thoughtful design balanced hard surfaces with soft colors.

"Yes, hard to believe right? I mean for a man with such a limited vocabulary and all." His mouth twitched at one end into a wry grin.

Her cheeks grew hot. She wanted to reach out and pinch him—hard—but that wouldn't help her secure a place to stay, so she smiled and reached inside herself for the apology he deserved and no doubt expected.

"I'm sorry, that wasn't what I meant. Few people use the word *ambidextrous*. Usually they'll say something like 'I have to learn to use my other hand' or something like that. It wasn't a personal affront despite how it sounded."

"Apology accepted." Wes smiled and her knees turned to Jell-O with the way they wobbled. He was not her type, but something about him attracted her. She didn't know if it was the raw male energy that seemed to vibrate off him, or maybe it was that damn crooked smile. She had a thing for smiley faces after all. "What's the problem at the apartment over the bakery?"

She shuddered at the memory. "It has bees."

CHAPTER SIX

Wes's smile grew wider until it turned into a full-fledged laugh. "You bust my balls for not liking needles and you're afraid of a bee?"

Her cheeks turned from pink to crimson as her temper flared. He was taught to never poke a bear but teasing Lydia was fun. He liked the way she responded with bold authenticity.

"Yes, I'm deathly afraid of bees with an emphasis on *deathly*. While a shot to numb your pain or to prevent you from getting lockjaw won't kill you, a bee sting will put me six feet under if not treated immediately." She pulled the EpiPen from her purse and removed the protective cap to show him. As if training someone, she went through the motions of stabbing herself in leg without actually doing it.

Wes's pulse raced as the fear gripped him. Colors danced in front of his eyes. He blinked several times before they disappeared. There was no way he was going to the ground stone cold in front of Lydia again. A man could only take so many hits to his ego before considering himself damaged beyond repair. He white-knuckled the granite counter, not caring about the pain in his palm. "Got it. Now put that away."

To his relief, she capped it and tossed it back into her bag. As soon as it was gone, his breath resumed.

"What made you fear needles?"

He pushed off the counter and stood in front of her. Taller than her, he was positive if he leaned forward, he could rest his chin on her head. "No idea. We traveled a lot, and it started after I got a bunch of shots to go to Africa. I know it's an unreasonable fear, but I can't control it." In her eyes he saw understanding. "I'm sorry I judged you about the bees. That was insensitive."

She stared at him for a moment as if weighing his words on a truth scale. When she gave him a smile, he knew the scale had tipped in his favor. "Apology accepted."

"I think we got off to the wrong start." Wes held out his uninjured hand. "I'm Wes Covington."

"Nice to meet you, Wes. I'm Lydia Nichols."

"Let's get you a place to bunk, shall we?" He breezed past her. The smell of her fruity scent stopped him dead in his tracks. "Peach?"

She collided into his back and hugged him for balance.

"Excuse me?" Her hands lingered for a second, then dropped. "Sorry."

He spun around to face her. "Sorry that you ran into me or sorry that you felt me up and didn't press a dollar into my pants?"

"You stopped short. I had no warning."

Teasing her got a rise out of both. Only his happened in his pants while hers most likely had to do with her blood pressure.

"I smelled peaches." The smell brought him back to his

youth. Long before his father's expectations crushed his dreams.

"Good nose. It's my shampoo."

"Not really a good nose, just a good memory. I have two sisters and they went through a phase where everything they bought was fruit flavored or fruit scented down to the scratch-and-sniff stickers covering their bedroom walls. It was like living in a bowl of fruit cocktail. Peach was my favorite."

Lydia's laughter filled the air. The sound was sweeter than her peach shampoo.

"It's my favorite too." She gave the entry another look as if searching for something. "Do you live here by yourself?"

He shook his head. "No, Sarge lives here too. In fact, he's sleeping in your bed. He likes to sleep there during the day because your room gets the morning sun. We can just kick him out."

She followed him up the stairs. "I'm not kicking your roommate out."

Wes laughed. "He won't mind. He'll find himself another place in the house that suits him."

At the top of the stairs he turned down the hallway that led to six bedrooms. Only two had beds. He hadn't fully furnished the place since he bought it last year.

They'd made it halfway down the hall when a ball of fur shot in their direction like lead from a cannon. Sarge bypassed Wes and plowed straight into Lydia. She fell to her ass while the dog greeted her with sloppy wet kisses.

"Sarge! Nein! Sitz!" The dog gave Wes a mutinous look. Odd for Sarge since he'd lived a regimented life until his retirement two years ago, but he backed down and sat next to Lydia. When Wes offered his good hand to help her up, a low growl vibrated deep in Sarge's throat. "Nein!" Wes warned.

"Was he growling at me or you?" Lydia wiped the dog drool from her cheek.

Sarge sat at attention, his body placed between Wes and her. "I'd like to say he was growling at you, but I've seen that look on him and it would appear you've made a friend."

"What will he think of me when I steal his bed?" She fluffed the dog's furry head as they started down the hallway. "I suppose I could share with him. It's not like men are standing in line waiting to get into my bed."

That comment stunned him. He turned to face her. "I find that hard to believe. You're a beautiful woman."

"Flattery. Your sisters taught you well."

"My sisters taught me nothing. I speak the truth. You're an attractive woman. Even my dog likes you better than me."

The musical sound of her laugher floated down the narrow hallway. "He wants to sleep in my bed."

Sarge isn't the only one. That thought came from nowhere. Sure, Lydia was pretty, but she wasn't his type. She already had a foot out of the town he would always call home. That was a deal breaker. Nothing deep and lasting could come from a woman who dreamed a different dream. Been there, done that, and he didn't want a repeat.

He stepped into the second bedroom from the end. "Here's your bed. It's not much, but the last time I checked we were bee free." He pointed to a connecting door. "We have to share a bathroom. I haven't updated the one across the hallway yet and the one downstairs only has a working sink." He stepped to the door. "Do you need help with bags?"

"Valet service?" She walked around the room, which

had a queen bed, a dresser, and nothing else. "How much is rent?"

Wes leaned on the doorjamb and crossed one booted foot over the other. "Let's call it payment for services rendered."

"I'd really like to pay."

He raised his bandaged hand in the air. "You already did, but if you want to help with some projects until this heals, I can find something to keep you busy." Despite his best efforts to keep it clean, the once white gauze looked like it had been dragged through the mud.

"What the hell, Wes." She walked over and took his hand in hers. "Kitchen, now, and bring the bag of supplies Sage gave you." She breezed past him into the hallway.

He was still leaning on the doorframe when the sound of her shoes tapping down the wooden staircase filled the silence. He knew when she hit the bottom because he hadn't had time to fix the creak. Lydia had been in his house for ten minutes and she'd already taken over.

Sarge bounced on his feet, moving back and forth looking uncertain of where his loyalties should lie. Stay with Wes or go to her? "I'm the one that feeds you, buddy." The dog gave him one last look and raced after Lydia. "Traitor," he called after the dog.

After a quick stop in his room to get a flannel shirt, Wes went to the kitchen. If she were as observant as he thought, she'd have found the supplies on the little café table in the corner.

He rounded the corner to see Lydia at the sink scrubbing her hands the same way he did when they were covered in paint. Sarge lay at her feet.

"How is it you have any skin left?"

She soaped and washed several more times before she

turned off the water and dried her hands with paper towels. "You get used to it. I'd hate for someone to get a staph infection because I failed to thoroughly wash my hands. I control what I can and hope for the best with the rest. Now take a seat."

"You're a pushy little thing."

A shrug lifted her shoulders. "Only with stubborn children and obstinate men. I haven't decided which category you fit in yet."

Wes mimicked a dagger to his heart. "I'm wounded."

"You're in luck. I'm a doctor." She lifted a perfectly shaped brow. "Scissors?"

He nodded to the drawers behind her. "Top drawer on the left."

She rummaged inside. "Nope."

"Try the right."

A moment later. "Nope. Let's add disorganized to the mix. Hold on." She ran down the hallway and out the front door with Sarge trailing her. She returned a moment later with a duffel bag and her computer.

When she opened the bag, Wes realized it was a first-aid kit. The biggest he'd ever seen. Lydia had enough supplies for a small disaster. "You're like a Boy Scout."

"Yep, except I don't have a penis." Back at the sink she washed her hands again, then put on a pair of gloves.

"Still afraid you'll catch something?" He put his hand on the table palm side up. She took her scissors and cut the soiled bandage away.

"I'm not the one with an open wound." She'd turned his small table into a clinic and cleaned his injury. "You need to keep this clean. I'd hate to have to give you a shot because it got infected." Compassion peeked out between the cracks of her stern disposition.

Wes ignored her comment about the shot and looked at the finely stitched cut. "How many stitches did I get?" Her touch was soft and light. Was the tough act a shell she wore for a purpose?

"It was a significant wound." Her fingers brushed the crosshatched thread. "Twelve."

"I was a suture virgin before you came along," he teased.

"And I popped your cherry." She ran a layer of salve over the stitches and reapplied the bandage. "Stay out of the mud."

"Will do." The soft white gauze glowed against his tanned, work-roughened hands. "What, no Life Saver?" That was the best part about seeing Doc Parker. Wes was of the mind that if he had to suffer through treatment, he was entitled to a reward.

"You too?" She picked up a pen and drew a smiley face on his hand. "This will have to do for now."

"I feel cheated."

"Life Savers go to paying patients."

While she gathered her supplies, he searched for the scissors, which he found in the silverware drawer. "Here they are." He held them up.

"Day late and a dollar short," she replied.

"It's always the dollars with you." In his experience, women came from one of three camps. There were those who loved money, those who loved fame, and those who loved themselves. Lydia at this point belonged to camp one.

"Speaking of dollars, I need to get back to the job hunt. Do you have internet?"

Yep, group number one. "Password is *myperfectworld*. All lower case with no spaces." He opened the top drawer on the left and tossed the scissors where they belonged.

She glanced around the kitchen. "Take this house and

put it in Cherry Creek or Colorado Springs and I'd agree that it's a perfect world, but Aspen Cove? Not setting your sights high, are you?"

That statement confirmed why he could have nothing more than friendship with Lydia. Her priorities were skewed.

He leaned against the sink and stared at her. She was beautiful, but when she smiled, there was no sparkle in her eyes. Wes recognized that look. It was the look of discontentment. He'd seen it in the mirror every morning when he put on his coat and tie and went to the office. He didn't miss that life.

Leaving the family business had been the hardest thing he'd ever done. The scowl etched into his father's face was burned into his memory. As the only son, he was the golden child, and he'd done what was expected until the expectations noosed tightly around his neck and threatened to strangle him.

He'd disappointed many people, but it came down to them versus him. That one moment of selfishness changed his life and his outlook on the world. He loved his family, but Aspen Cove was where he belonged. "My sights are fine. My life is perfect. What about yours, Lydia? When was the last time you were truly happy?"

CHAPTER SEVEN

Lydia didn't know whether to laugh or cry. It was laughable that a man as good-looking and seemingly intelligent as Wes could find his bliss in a town as small as Aspen Cove. Heartbreaking that he could see her misery when she tried so hard to mask it with a smile.

"Who says I'm not happy." She gave him a smile her orthodontist would have used for an ad. "This smile doesn't lie."

"I'll believe you when that smile reaches those beautiful blues of yours." He pushed off the sink and walked toward the hall. Over his shoulder he said, "I'll be out front if you need me." He looked at Sarge whose snout nuzzled her feet. "You coming, boy?"

When the dog ignored him, Wes turned and left. The last thing she heard was him mumbling something about loyalty.

"My priorities are fine," she said to no one, but she was used to talking to air. She'd spent the past few months talking to herself. Too bad her self-counsel hadn't been effective.

Lydia sat in silence and thought about his question. When was the last time she was truly happy? Surely it couldn't have been that long ago. When she pressed her memory, all she came up with was the day she started her residency and found out Dr. McKay would be her mentor. He'd saved her life. From that point on, her happiness was woven tightly to his. Sadly, she was a convenient option for him, not a choice.

When his apartment building caught fire, she happily offered him a place to live. When he told her he hated scheduling the staff, she did it for him. He hadn't loved her, only what she did for him. After their breakup, she realized everything she missed about him hadn't been there in the first place.

She knew what happiness looked like for everyone else, but only had a vague outline of what it looked like for herself.

She opened her computer and typed in the password for Wi-Fi. Wasn't it time she went after her perfect world—a world that offered a top position in an urban emergency room? Where days off included friends and wine. Where the right man saw her for what she offered the world not what she offered him. Maybe a perfect world wasn't obtainable, but she'd settle for pretty damn close and that meant she needed a job.

Three hours later she was still at the kitchen table when Wes walked in bare-chested and sexy as hell. He had a body fine-tuned by hard labor. She hated to compare every man to Adam, but he was the only man she could use as a reference. Side-by-side there would be no similarity. Adam was fit but in a healthy diet sort of way. Wes was exercise art, carved from stone or forged from steel.

"Still searching for the dream?" Sweat dripped from his

brow. He lifted the faucet handle and ducked his head under the stream of water. When he stood, droplets splashed everywhere with one hitting her cheek. "Sorry about that." He pulled two clean towels from a nearby drawer and tossed one her way. Once he'd dried his face, he chucked the wet towel into the pile in the corner. "I finally got that window aligned and didn't need more stitches."

"Hard to believe those were your first." She couldn't take her eyes off his chest. A light smattering of hair trailed down and disappeared into the waistband of his worn jeans. Jeans that hung precariously low from his hips. One tug and they'd lie in a pool of denim at his feet. She shook the thought from her head and brought her eyes to his face.

His tongue slipped out to catch a drop of water on his lip. "For firsts, you were really good." The damn man winked at her and she nearly fell from her chair. What the hell was wrong with her? She had put a kibosh on men for now. Besides, Wes wasn't even her type. She liked tall, dark and dashing. He was tall, fair, and oh so fine.

"You okay?" He looked at her like she'd gone pale; impossible with the way his heat swirled around her.

"Why wouldn't I be?"

His face scrunched up like a shar-pei. "Your face looks like this."

"My face does not look like that." She adjusted the screen of her computer so she could see her reflection. He was right. She'd frowned so deeply her eyebrows nearly touched.

He turned his back and opened the refrigerator. "You hungry?"

A glance at his broad back had her nodding. "For food?" slipped out without thought. "Yes, I'm hungry." She needed to get herself under control. One look at a half-naked man made her mouth water, and food was the last thing on her mind. "All I had was a muffin, and that was hours ago."

He shut the door and turned around. "Let me get a clean shirt and I'll take you to the diner."

She wanted to tell him not to bother with the shirt, but Maisey wouldn't let him inside without one. "Sounds great." *God help me.*

He wasn't gone longer than a minute. When he returned, he wore a bright yellow T-shirt that clung to him like a second skin. She fought the urge to grab a Sharpie and draw a happy face across his chest. Eyes at his nipples and a mouth skimming the edge of his jeans would be perfect.

That thought left when Wes did. He moved down the hallway with purposeful steps, his boots beating a path to the front door. "You coming?" he called.

She rushed after him. When Sarge tried to follow, Wes got down on his knees and explained that dogs weren't allowed in the diner. He said he'd take him to the bar later to visit Otis. Sarge lowered his head and wilted into the hardwood floor.

"You think he understood you?"

"Animals are a lot smarter than we think. He has a big vocabulary. I read somewhere that dogs can memorize hundreds of words." Wes bent down and fluffed the fur on his head. "Sarge is bilingual." He smiled at Lydia. "Another word you might be surprised I know." Though he said it in jest, she felt bad he said it at all.

"How many times will I have to say I'm sorry?"

"I think a dozen or more should do it."

Wes set his left hand on the small of her back and walked her to his truck. Like a gentleman, he opened the door and helped her inside.

"I can drive," she said after he rounded the truck and

climbed behind the wheel.

He laughed, the sound so warm it felt like warm syrup drizzling over her body.

"My poor ego couldn't take it." With the push of a button, the diesel's engine growled, throaty and loud.

"Your ego should be solid. Look at you. Handsome with a killer body and passable personality." She couldn't help herself with Wes. He was fun to tease.

"Passable, huh?" He backed out of the driveway and headed the few blocks to Main Street. "My self-esteem hit the ground when I did. I saw that needle and down I went. Can't say I'm not embarrassed by that."

"Trypanophobia is nothing to be ashamed about. Up to ten percent of the population hates needles enough to pass out. Your faint made it easier to treat the injury. So thank you for that."

He reached over and laid his bandaged hand on top of hers. "Thanks, Doc. Maybe your bedside manner isn't so bad after all."

"At least you didn't liken me to the devil."

His eyes grew wide as he pulled into an open parking space in front of the diner. "Not out loud anyway."

She yanked her hand from under his and pinched the area of skin at the side of his ribs. She laughed when he squealed like a baby. "Come on, you wimp, I'll buy you lunch." She hopped out of his truck.

"Not on your life, sweetheart. I don't want to hear about how you had to bandage me up and feed me. Lunch is on me."

"Fine, but I'm warning you, I eat like a lumberjack."

"I can handle it. I can handle anything you throw at me."

Was that a challenge? She never could pass up a challenge. "Game on."

They entered the almost empty diner, not unusual since it was past the normal lunch hour. Maisey rushed over with an iced tea for Wes and a questioning look for Lydia.

"If you were a regular, she'd have known what to bring already," Wes said.

"I'll have the same."

When Maisey left, she asked, "Doesn't regular get boring? Do you ever change your mind and want something different?"

"Sure, I like to try new things, but it's nice when someone knows you well enough to know what you prefer. I always drink tea. Never much cared for soda. At the bar, I always drink dark beer. I can't explain it, but these people are the family I choose. They get me."

"Sage is all the family I've got." She couldn't believe they were the last of their line.

"Family isn't only who you're born to but includes who you choose."

Lydia had spent little time building a family outside her sister and wondered what a family looked like to Wes. "Tell me about yours."

Maisey placed a glass of iced tea in front of Lydia and took their orders. They both asked for blue-plate specials. Today was meatloaf and mashed potatoes. She had to admit there was comfort in knowing what she ordered would be what she wanted.

"You met Agatha. She's my mom's aunt."

"She's a Guild, right? Your house is called the Guild House. Is it a family property?"

He sat taller. The house made him proud. "Yes, it was the first house ever built in Aspen Cove. My family has deep roots here. My great grandfather Thomas Guild moved here over a century ago. He, Isaiah Bennett and Rushton Parker came here looking for gold. They never found it, but did okay in logging and then manufacturing."

History fascinated Lydia. "So, Rushton is an ancestor of Doc's, and Isaiah is related to Bea Bennett?"

"You're almost right. Rushton was Doc's grandfather. Isaiah was Bea's grandfather-in-law, so her husband's side of the family. He was a builder like me. He built the Guild House. The Parkers weren't always in medicine. Doc is the first in his family to be a healer. His grandfather raised livestock in the valley between the peaks. You'll have to get him to tell you how he won Phyllis's heart by butchering his prize hog."

"Does Doc have any children?" Lydia sipped her tea. "No one has mentioned any." She looked up to see the frown on Wes's face.

"Yes, he has a daughter, but she stopped talking to him the day Phyllis died."

Maisey arrived with their specials. Lydia looked at the plate overflowing with home-cooked goodness and had to admit she wouldn't mind meatloaf every Thursday.

After her first delicious bite, she urged Wes to continue. "Why would she disown him?"

"Doc is bigger than life in this town. Kind of a hero in these parts. He's book brilliant and timeless, but when Phyllis had a stroke, he couldn't save her, and Charlotte—or Charlie as everyone calls her—couldn't handle it. She looked up to him like he hung the moon. Like somehow he was capable of anything. Phyllis's death made him mortal."

Lydia set her fork down. "That's unfair. You can't save them all no matter how hard you try. Poor Doc."

Wes ate the way he kept house. There was no plan. He mixed it all together until total chaos covered his plate.

"Agatha is working to mend the fences between father and daughter."

"His daughter must be in her fifties. She should know better." Lydia picked up her fork and stabbed a bite of meatloaf. She moved clockwise around her plate, taking bites of everything in order.

"She's actually not much older than you and me. She's in her thirties. They had her later in life with the help of modern medicine. Phyllis was in her late forties when Charlie was born."

"Wow." Lydia couldn't imagine having a child in her forties. She was rounding the corner to thirty-three and considered herself almost on the shelf. With no father prospects, she was unlikely to have children and would have to be happy being aunt to Sage's future children.

"Doc is family to everyone. It doesn't take DNA to be part of a family."

"You have sisters, but what about brothers?"

"I'm the only boy."

"I bet your sisters spoiled you."

"Terrorized me was more like it."

When they finished, Maisey picked up their plates and asked about pie. Wes declined, but Lydia ordered cherry. The last time she had a piece was at her sister's engagement party. She hadn't stopped at one. She'd eaten a whole pie straight from the tin.

"You're not kidding about eating like a lumberjack. How do you keep that body, eating so many calories?"

She ran her hands down her sides like a game show host showing off an appliance. "You like this body?"

"Looks better on you then it would have on the devil."

"You want me to pinch you again?"

He pressed himself against the booth to gain distance.

"No, I want to know how you can consume that much food and not waddle out of the diner."

"Hollow leg," she said in a serious tone. When he rolled his eyes, she added, "I have a killer metabolism. I'm sure it will turn around at some point, but my body is still programmed to work thirty-six-hour shifts and live off espresso."

"What are you going to do now that you're on a regular schedule?"

"Regular? Who works two days on and has five days off?"

Maisey brought the pie. "Me in the winter," she chimed in. She tore the check off the pad and placed it in front of Wes. "I love the winter schedule."

Lydia forked a big bite of pie into her mouth while Wes handed Maisey thirty dollars and told her to keep the change. The bill wasn't over twenty bucks. It made Lydia happy to see Wes wasn't a cheap bastard. Adam would have pulled out his calculator to figure fifteen percent to the penny.

"Is Dalton in the back?" Wes asked.

Maisey shook her head. "Are you kidding? I've never seen that boy clean up a kitchen so fast and disappear. Now that Samantha's here I have the tidiest kitchen in town. Ben took over the second shift so if you want something else let me know." She disappeared into the kitchen.

"Can't blame Dalton." Lydia scraped the last of the filling from the plate and licked her fork clean. "I don't play for the V team, but if I did, Samantha would have my vote too."

Wes choked on his tea. "You met her?"

"Oh yeah, we go way back to a few weeks ago when I visited my sister. The same week I got suckered into covering for Doc. I like her. For being richer than Oprah, she's down to earth."

Wes stood and offered Lydia his hand. She took it, and a tingle from his touch raced all the way to her core. They exited the diner and stood on the sidewalk out front, where several people were milling about.

"No one's as rich as Oprah, but that girl has her priorities straight. She put Dalton first."

Lydia pulled her hand from his. "Why would you say that? Does a woman have to give up everything to get her priorities straight?"

He gave her a look. The kind a person got when they knew someone was speaking their language but it sounded foreign. "No, all I'm saying is she found what made her happy and took the steps to secure it."

"Not all of us are wealthy enough to build our dream center like she can."

Wes gave her the same look her father had when he was disappointed. "If you think the center makes her happy, you're not as smart as I first thought."

Her inner child lashed out. "Well, you're not as cute as I first thought either." Lydia wanted to crawl into a hole and die. She was far beyond playground games, yet Wes made her feel so small when he pointed out the obvious. She knew without a doubt Samantha would have given up everything to be with Dalton because he was the key component to her perfect world.

"You think I'm cute?" He opened the passenger side door for her, but she walked past him toward her sister's place.

"I don't know what I think anymore. All I know is I can't think around you. I'm going to my sister's."

The echo of his laughter chased her down Main Street.

CHAPTER EIGHT

Wes laughed all the way home. Something told him his life as he knew it would change as long as Lydia was in town.

Sarge greeted him at the door.

"Oh, so now you want to be my dog again?" Did he see remorse in the dog's eyes or was that hunger? The shepherd put his nose to work and found his treat tucked inside Wes's back pocket. "You're nothing but a treat whore. What am I going to do with you?" The bigger question was what would he do about Lydia. Before he could think too much about the pretty blonde with a killer ass, the doorbell rang.

Obviously, she'd changed her mind and had walked home. He swung the door open and said, "So I *am* as cute as you thought." The last word caught in his throat. Standing on his doorstep were four men big enough to be linebackers.

The man in front spoke first. "Not really my type, but I suppose you'd catch someone's eye." He offered Wes his hand. "I'm Noah Lockhart." He turned around. "These are my brothers, Ethan, Bayden, and Quinn. We had a meeting."

He really needed to get his schedule straight. "Shit.

Sorry. I thought you were someone else. Someone of the female persuasion."

All four men glanced at their zippers and said, "Nope," like they were a single entity. It was funny to see siblings in action. His sisters were the same. Get them in a room together and they could finish each other's sentences. When they were in high school, they often came downstairs for breakfast wearing the same outfit. Born nine months apart, Mom called them Irish twins even though they weren't Irish.

"Come on in."

Sarge walked around the men as if sniffing for contraband or maybe looking for milk bones.

"That's Sarge, he's harmless unless you pack heat or drugs. If that's the case, you'll most likely lose a limb."

Ethan looked down at Wes's hand. "Learn that firsthand?"

"Nah, I had a fight with a window sash. The sash won."

The men looked at his home. He saw the appreciation in their eyes when they took in the restoration work that had been completed.

"Are you refurbishing this house on your own?" Noah asked.

Wes led them to the dining room, where Dalton had left the rolled-up plans to the Guild Center. "I had help, but with the growth here in Aspen Cove, I've had to move my crews around. I'm short on qualified builders. That's where I hope you'll come in. Can I get you a drink? I've got water or beer."

Noah, who seemed to be the one in charge, said they'd take water. Wes didn't mind if his crew had a beer at the end of the day. He often supplied a cooler full or bought the first round at Bishop's Brewhouse, but it was good to see the

Lockharts were on the same page and asked for water while working. That showed a sense of professionalism he appreciated.

He grabbed five ice-cold bottles and returned to the dining room table, where he found the men sitting and staring at the rolled-up architectural drawings.

"Go ahead, have a look."

Quinn was the first to reach for the plans. His smile grew when he flattened them on the table. The brothers set their water bottles on the four corners and stood above the pages.

"Who's the designer?" Bayden asked.

"I am. The building belonged to my ancestors. It was important to respect the history while bringing the building into this century." Wes skimmed the plans and smiled. He took great pride in the work he did. He'd designed a building that would pay homage to his ancestors and still provide modern amenities to its new occupants. There had to be a balance between old and new.

"You're going green with solar power and recycled materials," Noah remarked. "I like that. We recently completed a large project in Fury for a development called Abundance. They went green too. Reviving small towns is where it's at."

"I'm on the fence as to how revived I'd like to see Aspen Cove. I like it small, but I see the need for infrastructure and upgrades."

Wes spent the next two hours going over the plans. He was impressed with the Lockharts. They knew what they were doing. Each of the brothers had a specialty from electrical to plumbing. As they wrapped up their meeting, Sarge barked and took off down the hallway. Seconds later there was a screech and a crash.

All five men rushed toward the sound of chaos. Lying in the entry surrounded by spilled produce was Lydia. No matter how much she struggled she couldn't stop Sarge from licking her face. Finally, she screamed "Sitz!" The dog obeyed.

Noah reached out a hand before Wes could offer his, and helped Lydia to her feet. He didn't like the way Noah looked at her. Wasn't happy with how she smiled at him and said thanks in her sweetest voice.

She rubbed her bottom. "That dog is a nuisance." Though she pointed at Sarge, her eyes were on Wes. "Seriously, he's going to kill me before the day is over." She looked from man to man until she'd made the rounds and her eyes came back to Wes. "Look at the mess he made." She bent over and picked up the apples and oranges that rolled from her bag.

"Are you all going to stand there while that beast eats everything?" By the door Sarge gobbled up an apple. "I'll never understand men." She gathered the spilled produce, picked up the bag, and walked past them into the kitchen. Like moths to a flame they followed her. She pulled a big bowl from the cupboard and filled it with the fruit.

"Do you have more bags that need to come inside?" Bayden asked.

"No, this was it but thank you for asking. At least one of you has some manners."

Wes stepped in front of the brothers. "Lydia, these are the Lockharts." He pointed to each one and said their name.

All four brothers stepped forward to shake her hand. Noah turned to Wes. "Your taste in women and projects are both excellent."

Lydia's *pffft* sound turned their heads. "I'm not his woman. Can't you see? The dog has claimed me." Sitting by her side was Sarge. "I'm Lydia Nichols, and I'm temporarily filling in for Doc Parker while he recovers."

The brothers nodded. News of the fire had spread quickly. There wasn't a person within a hundred-mile radius who hadn't heard about Samantha and her arsonist manager. Now there wouldn't be a person within that same radius who wouldn't know about the hot little doctor in Aspen Cove. Wes wasn't sure how he felt about that. All he knew was there was something raw and vulnerable about her. It showed in the way she strapped on her armor.

"Awful thing," they all mumbled.

Lydia turned and continued to put her groceries away while the five men stared at her. Six if Wes counted the dog. She looked at them and said, "Are you waiting for your smiley face sticker or what?" She reached into her bag and took several packages of stickers out. She tore the plastic off one pack and put a sticker on each man's shirt. When she got to Wes, he held up the hand that still had the inked face she drew earlier.

"I'm good. I've got an original." He turned toward the Lockharts. "Looks like we've been dismissed. I'll see you guys tomorrow at the site. We'll start with demolition and go from there." Wes walked them to the door and came back to the kitchen to find Lydia frowning in front of her computer.

He pulled two beers from the refrigerator and popped the caps before he handed her one. "You turned four badass construction workers into six-year-old boys wondering how they could earn their next sticker."

She brought the beer to her lips and took a long drink. The furrow between her brows relaxed. Her frown flipped into a smile. "Only four of them?"

"Sarge doesn't care about stickers."

"What about you? I don't imagine you're a sticker kind of guy either." Her eyes lifted from her screen to him.

Those damn steely blue/gray eyes that took his breath away. Plump pink lips that guaranteed hours of memorable kisses. A body that could rock his world. Why did he always want what was bad for him?

"Stickers don't really do it for me." He pulled out a chair and sat across from her.

"Me either, but you should have seen Bailey Brown's mom when I drew on her hand."

Wes was familiar with the Browns. He'd helped Hank build a smokehouse a few months ago and caught Bailey when she fell from the rafters. That little girl was a precocious little daredevil. "I imagine her mom's head spun and she spit green soup. Cassidy Brown is a perfect example of a tiger mom, or maybe a helicopter parent."

"Most likely tiger mom. No way is she a helicopter parent unless her flight path was off that day because that kid managed to shove a perfectly good Skittle up her nose."

"Bailey takes after her father. Big balls, little brains. He once poked a grizzly to see if he could outrun it." Wes would never forget that day.

"Oh my God, what happened?"

"I was fishing in the cove when Hank Bailey ran past me butt naked. Not a sight I'd wish on my worst enemy." He leaned forward like he was telling a secret. "He dropped his clothes as he ran into the water hoping the bear would lose his scent. Turns out the bear kept his scent all right, but wasn't interested in a man who showered only on Sundays."

Her face twisted. "Yuck. Seriously? No wonder Bailey popped that Skittle into her mouth without thought. No sense of hygiene." Lydia tipped back her beer and gulped like she was trying to wash the taste of something bad away. "Cassidy looked like she bathed."

"They're good people. They're off-the-gridders who live up in the mountains in a rustic cabin. Hard to shower daily when you don't have running water."

"Why would someone want to live like that?"

"Different people want different things. What do you want, Dr. Nichols? Seems to me that you're not quite satisfied with your life."

She closed her eyes and scrubbed her face with her palms. "I've hit a few stumbling blocks recently."

Wes pressed his finger against her laptop, closing it with one push so he could get a better look at her. She appeared tired, or was that a look of resignation in her eyes?

"Want to talk about it?" He was a good sounding board, a skill he'd learned from hard lessons. His whole life his father told him to listen, but he never seemed to heed his own advice. Talking to Nick Covington was like talking to a wall. Wes had made a promise to himself that if someone ever needed an ear, he'd give them both of his.

Her neck popped as she rotated it. Long blond hair floated over her shoulders and curled at the top of her breasts. Breasts Wes knew without a doubt would be the perfect mouthful. Her pink T-shirt dipped just enough to show the milky white perfection of her skin.

She rolled the cold glass bottle over the exposed part of her chest. He wondered if she realized how hot that was, or if she felt her nipples tighten under his gaze.

Focus, man. You're here to listen.

"You ever feel like you're swimming upstream?" She finished the beer and slid the empty across the table.

He got her a fresh one and moved his seat closer to hers. "I used to but not anymore."

"What changed?"

"My priorities." Wes peeled the label from the bottle. When he was a kid, he and his friends believed if they could get the label off without tearing it, they'd get lucky. It never actually happened, but a guy could dream. He inched it free without a single tear and lifted it in the air like a trophy.

She swiped it from his fingers and shredded it to pieces. "You still believe that works?"

Wes chuckled. "Never has before. Are you offering to up my success ratio?"

She tossed the paper into the air. Gold confetti floated down around them.

"Sounds like you have my kind of luck."

He sipped his beer and took a long hard look at her.

"I believe we make our own luck." His stomach growled. "You hungry? I'm going to throw a pizza in the oven. You're welcome to share it with me."

"Frozen pizza?" Lydia groaned. "Sounds like you got the same culinary training as my sister." She stood, walked to the refrigerator, and pulled out a few items she'd brought home from the store. "I'll make dinner while you tell me how I go about changing my luck."

She threw ingredients together into a frying pan. He had no idea what she was making, but it smelled good.

"There is no such thing as luck in my mind. There are only choices. If the choices you make aren't right for you, then your life might seem unlucky."

"So you're saying because I'm unhappy my choices were bad. My choice to be a doctor wasn't a good choice?" She turned down the heat and covered the pan before she came back to her beer and her chair.

"No, that's not what I said. When you're at work, are you happy?"

She pulled her legs to her chest and rested her chin on her knees. Lydia Nichols didn't look like the formidable physician who'd intimidated him into an unmanly swoon. She appeared childlike and uncertain.

"Not everyone is happy every minute of the day, but yes, when I'm helping people get healthy, I feel happy."

"Were you happy when you helped me?"

She looked at his still clean bandage. "Yes, helping you made me happy."

He smiled. "Glad I could be of service." He liked her being happy around him.

"It's more than the work. I invested years to become a doctor. You're right, I made a bad choice." She cocked her head. "A few of them actually, and now I'm paying the price."

"Okay, so poor choices lead to unhappiness."

"Right." With the neck of the beer bottle pinched between her fingers while she swung it back and forth, she opened and closed her mouth several times as if debating her words. "Sleeping with my boss was a bad choice."

Wes didn't expect that. This wasn't *Taxicab Confessions*, but the subject intrigued him. What kind of woman was Lydia? "Your boss?"

"It's a long story, but in college he saved my life. You know, the bee sting issue. When I showed up for residency, it seemed like providence. He was my mentor, and well...things happened. Then it went to hell."

He sat back and digested that information. "Older man?"

"Yes, by ten years." She brought her beer to her lips. "That's not my thing. It just happened to be that Adam was older. I was so enamored with him and the initial attention he gave me."

"What happened?" He already knew the story or at least guessed it. There was no doubt Lydia was not Adam's first or his last workplace fling.

"He wasn't forthcoming with me. He held back and didn't communicate. He walked in and out of my heart like it had a revolving door. He took advantage of what I offered. He freeloaded until he had enough money to buy a house and get a new girlfriend. The worst part was I thought I'd get a position in the ER at Denver General based on my skills, but I was overlooked based on our breakup. Turns out I didn't really know him at all."

"All right, so you didn't get the job. Could you imagine working in the same department with him for years after a breakup? If you're a believer in luck, not getting hired seems lucky."

"He wouldn't even give me a reference, which is killing my chance at securing a job elsewhere."

"Why? I'd think he'd be happy to give you a reference to get you out of his hair."

She rose from the chair to stir the meal that smelled way better than the collective ingredients of chicken and vegetables should.

When she turned around her face was red. Wes wasn't sure if it was from the beer, the heat of the stove, or what she would tell him next.

She fisted her hands on her hips and jutted one side out. "I've had a moment or two when things aren't clear in my head, and I say or do things inappropriate for my age."

He remembered her comment about him not being cute. That was adorable because Wes knew every human had an inside child in need of nurturing. He'd run into his inner six-year-old many times without warning.

"What did you do? Tell him he wasn't as cute as you used to think?"

She took a deep breath. "Never living that down, am I? You know, the more you remind me of my missteps, the less cute you become."

"At least I'm still cute."

She pulled her lower lip between her teeth. "Yes, you are, but it was worse than that." She reached for her beer. This was a deep drink confession. "I had a picture of his junk and posted it in the lounge with the title *I'm a dick*."

"Did it make you feel better?"

She gave him an are-you-crazy look. "It was awesome until people facebooked, instagrammed, and tweeted it. Adam McKay's franks and beans went viral."

"I can't imagine having your junk go viral is a bad thing unless..."

She nodded. She held her fingers six inches apart and closed the gap to three. "Fully erect."

"Ouch. So what's your priority right now?"

Again she gave him a duh look. "Right now I need plates." She went back to the pan and pulled it from the burner. "Long-term, I need a job."

"You have a job. I'll get you plates."

He reached over her head for two dinner plates. The smell of her shampoo filled his nose. God, he liked peaches.

"Working as a country doctor is not my dream job." She dished up a chicken breast and a healthy serving of vegetables in some kind of creamy sauce. "If you could do anything, would you be here refurbishing houses?"

Without reservation, he said, "Yes. This is exactly what I want to do."

"You're lucky then."

He took both plates back to the table. "I told you it's not luck. It's choices."

She plopped onto her chair and forked a carrot. "You're impossible."

Before he took a bite of what he knew would be the best meal he'd eaten in a long time, he said, "Yep, but don't forget I'm cute."

CHAPTER NINE

Sweat drenched her T-shirt. Hair tickled her nose. Lydia's eyes popped open when a body moved beside her. Staring her in the face was Sarge, who'd snuck into her room last night.

"Get off me, you beast." She pushed at him, but the more she tried to move him, the more determined he was to stay. "Fine, you can stay for a few more minutes and then we have to get up." One glance at her phone showed it was after ten. Never had she slept so late without coming off a double shift. Maybe it was the fresh Colorado air or the three beers she had while exposing her soul to Wes.

The man had sat and listened to her for an hour. While he offered his opinion about her lot in life, it never came out as judgmental. He delivered his insights through thought-provoking questions—questions she'd asked herself like what made her happy. If the world ceased to exist tomorrow, what would be her biggest regret?

"What about you, Sarge? If today was your last day, what would you do with it?" The dog stretched and moved in closer to coat her face with kisses.

She laughed and buried her head under the blanket. "Just like a man."

In the distance, Wes called out Sarge's name. The dog waited until he heard his owner say, "Come and eat," before he bolted from her bed.

Lydia threw off the covers and climbed out of bed. "Yep, just like a man all right. Food first, women second."

She walked into the bathroom, which smelled like citrus and pine. The adjoining door was cracked open. She shouldn't snoop but couldn't help herself. Wes confused her. He was everything she never wanted and yet he'd filled her thoughts since the moment she'd met him.

When she opened the door fully, she wasn't surprised to find an unmade bed and a pile of dirty clothes in the corner. A family picture sat on his dresser surrounded by change and gum wrappers. Wes wasn't conventional in his choices. Where most people would have some kind of mint, Wes's flavor choice was Juicy Fruit.

She picked up the photo of a younger Wes surround by who she assumed were his parents and sisters. Wes didn't have the fine lines around his eyes that he did these days—lines that didn't age him as much as enhance his features. Thankfully, he looked more like his mother than his father, whose scowl cast a shadow over the photo. She put it back and looked around the room.

Wes didn't have much in the way of furniture, but the room was beautiful with high ceilings and crown moldings. What he lacked in housekeeping skills he made up for with his restorative talents. This house was hundreds of years old. He could have taken the easy way out and modernized it, but it was obvious he loved bringing out the beauty of what was already in place.

She heard his footsteps on the stairs and rushed from his

room through the bathroom. Seconds later, there was a soft knock on her door.

Pretending like she hadn't been snooping, she messed up her hair and answered the door with a yawn as if she'd crawled out of bed seconds before.

"Good morning, Lydia." His eyes took her in from her tangled mess to her pink painted toenails. When his gaze stopped at her breasts on their way back up, she looked down to find her traitorous nipples pebbled and pointing at him.

She immediately crossed her arms over her chest. "Did you need something?"

His tongue swept across his lower lip, leaving it wet. "Just wanted to make sure you slept okay and to tell you if you don't want Sarge in your bed, you'll have to make sure your door clicks when you shut it. I saw he nudged it open at some point last night." Had he spied on her while she slept?

"Oh, yes. I woke up to a wet tongue and fur. Can't complain through. It's been a while since I woke up to kisses and a warm body." She giggled. How sad was it that the only man she could get into her bed was a dog who traded her without a thought for a bowl of kibble?

"I'm heading out to the paper mill. I've got the guys you met last night meeting me there."

"Are you working for them?" She heard them say something about meeting at the site.

Wes braced his hands on the doorframe. "Other way around. They work for me. I own Covington Construction."

She realized her mistake when his lips stretched into a thin line. She seemed to constantly underestimate him.

"Right, that makes sense." She glanced back at her room. "You do beautiful work."

He watched her for a second before he pulled his left hand down from the frame and opened it to reveal a key. "You'll probably need this." He pushed off the frame. "Help yourself to anything you want. I left the remote on the coffee table. There's a pot of fresh brewed coffee for you downstairs. Have a good day, Lydia."

She stepped into the hallway to watch him walk away. His jeans hugged his ass like a wet leather glove. He talked to her yesterday about choices. At this minute, she didn't have much choice but to stand in place and watch him disappear. To turn away from a body like that would have been disrespectful to the universe.

When the crown of his head disappeared down the stairs, she headed straight to the bathroom. While Wes had preserved the beauty of the house, he'd also upgraded. Multiple jets shot from the walls of the shower. She took five minutes to figure out how to run the thing, but when she stepped inside, she wasn't sure she'd ever leave. Wes might come home and find her naked and pruned, but she'd be happy.

Hot water pulsed over her body like masseuses' hands kneading her skin. The tension in her muscles didn't come from overexertion. It came from the weight of disappointment.

Since she'd left her overnight bag in the bathroom at the apartment, she lathered herself up with what was available. The smell of Wes's citrus body wash moved through the steamy air. She was covered in his scent by the time she stepped out to dry off.

Back on her bed was Sarge, who snuggled under the covers. "Out." She pointed to the door. "If you're not going to find me a job or make me breakfast, you don't get to sleep in my bed." When she stomped her bare foot on the hardwood floor, he jumped from the bed and slunk out the door.

Fifteen minutes later she found him curled under the kitchen table. Just as Wes promised, there was fresh coffee in the pot and a muffin on a plate in front. Lydia's heart skipped a beat at his thoughtfulness. Despite her less than pleasant demeanor the past few days, he'd opened his house to her and made her feel like she was welcome. That was a lot more than she could say for Adam.

Looking for a way to repay the kindness, she decided the one thing Wes needed more than anything was to have his kitchen cleaned.

She picked up the pile of towels from the corner and found the washer and dryer in a mudroom at the back of the house. As she dumped detergent into the tub and started the machine, she asked herself why she was doing this. Was it because she wanted to or because she felt she had to? Was it to make him happy or her?

She felt it was right to contribute something. She knew without a doubt if she left the pile there it would be there until no towels remained. Wes had no expectation of her cleaning his house. Maybe that was why she did it. It wasn't an obligation but an act of kindness returned for his hospitality. Returning the kindness made her happy.

The OCD in her couldn't stop there. By noon, she'd cleaned the kitchen, dusted the downstairs and was starting on alphabetizing the canned goods when her phone rang. She rushed to it hoping it was an employment call. Those hopes were dashed when she saw it was Sage.

"What's up?" Lydia answered.

"Just reminding you to come by the bar tonight and don't forget the ribbon cutting for the new park is tomorrow. We have to man the first aid tent."

She could live without the bar tonight, but the prospect of working tomorrow delighted her. It would at least eat some hours in her day. "Perfect. Glad to help, but do you really think we need a tent? It's a park."

"Better safe than sorry. Katie rented a bouncy castle and the Bishops are barbecuing. Either could be a recipe for disaster, but combine the two, and I can guarantee the need for Band-Aids."

"Sounds good. I've got my first aid kit in the car."

"I'll bring the one from the clinic. What are you doing today?"

"Oh, you know, just had a massage and waiting for a manicure and a pedicure. Thought I'd take in a movie and maybe lunch at the little Italian café down the street," she teased.

"So you're drinking coffee and job hunting."

Her sister knew her well. "Actually, that's on my agenda later. I had a massage in the most amazing shower, and I finished my third cup of coffee and the muffin Wes left for me." Lydia topped off her cup and walked to the cabinet where nothing made sense. It was a wonder the man found food at all. She picked up a can of soup that had expired six months ago and tossed it into the trash can. She'd replace everything she threw away.

"He made you coffee and bought you a muffin?"

"Sweet, huh?"

"I'd say. He's a good man. You know he stepped in when all that shit went down with Dalton. He power washed the graffiti off Dalton's house. No one asked him to do it, he just did. He also got his crew to bulldoze Samantha's burned down house. He's the one in charge of building the new firehouse and the Guild Center. I don't know how he does it all, but he seems to love it."

"Yes, weird, right? How a man as hot as Wes could be happy here."

Sage's growl came through loud and clear. "What does Wes being hot have to do with anything? He's happy because he's doing what he loves."

"So he told me. I wonder what he'll feel like in ten years when he's doing the same thing day in and day out. You think old Ray has few options in town? There doesn't seem to be much dating material for anyone north of twenty-five years old. Wes is screwed."

"Aspen Cove isn't the only pond to fish in. There's Copper Creek, Cross Creek, and Silver Springs."

"Oh, I never thought about other places. Does Wes have a girlfriend?" She hadn't considered the possibility. Aspen Cove made her farsighted. She couldn't see in front of her own eyes, let alone past the city limits.

"I have no idea. I don't know him that well." In the background, Otis barked. "Are you interested in him?"

Am I? The thought of time with Wes didn't repel her like most men did, but he wasn't like most men, or he didn't seem to be.

"He's nice, and I'll give him cute, but he's really not my type."

"Otis, get out of the water," her sister yelled. "Sorry, the damn dog is chasing birds into the lake. Back to Wes, it's a good thing he's not your type because your type hasn't been good for you." Sage had dried her tears for days when the end arrived. "You'll never know if you don't put yourself out there. You can't be a nun, that ship sailed the day you gave your V-card to Thomas O'Rourke, another lousy choice in men."

Sage was right. Thomas was cute, but that was all he'd

had going for him. "I'm leaving so there's no sense in getting involved with anyone."

Sage laughed. "I'm not asking you to marry him. He's a nice guy. What's the harm in having fun with a nice guy?"

"I'll think about it."

Another growl filled the silence. "That's your problem, you think too much. Come to the bar tonight. It's karaoke night. Everyone will be there."

"I said I'd think about it." She hated the frustrated tone she took with her sister.

"Stinking thinking," Sage said before she hung up and Lydia went back to organizing the pantry.

Wes had a lot of ready-made food. It was a wonder he was so solid and fit. She opened one of the six boxes of Pop-Tarts and put a pastry in the toaster. The least she could do was limit his simple carbohydrates by taking this treat off his hands.

When Sarge scratched at the back door, she let him into the fenced yard. Like the house, it was in the process of being refurbished with the flowerbeds tilled and waiting for planting, which couldn't begin until after Mother's Day due to the potential for frost.

A pergola sat white and pristine in the corner of the yard. Yellow and purple flowers poked their heads through the thawed ground, signaling spring in the Rockies had begun.

The yard would be beautiful when in full bloom. She could see herself sitting in a lounge chair reading a book. Sadness overcame her when she realized she'd never see this yard in its full glory. Wes's words came back to her about luck and choices. If luck shined on her, she'd be working hours away in Colorado Springs.

Sarge bounded back up the stairs and took his place at

her feet under the table. She nibbled on the strawberry pastry, chewing off the edges first and working her way into the sweet center. Her work in the kitchen was finished. Time to get back to her real life.

It was nearing five o'clock when she opened her computer. She scanned the forty emails that littered her mailbox.

Thunk

Her heart pounded when she saw an email from Memorial Hospital.

With the cursor hovering above the message, she debated opening it. The subject line gave nothing away. *Employment Inquiry* was all it said. Clicking would take liquid courage. No matter what the email said, her life would change forever. Hopefully it was a change for the better.

She rose and took the bottle of Chardonnay she'd bought yesterday from the now-clean refrigerator. Once she found the opener and a wineglass, she returned to her seat.

The cork popped and the *glug-glug* of the wine sounded as she splashed it into the glass. After one deep swallow, she opened the email and her entire life crumbled.

CHAPTER TEN

Wes entered the house expecting Sarge to race toward him for the treat he'd hidden in the laces of his boot, but his dog was nowhere in sight. If not for the whimpering coming from the kitchen, he would have thought the house was empty.

When the sound grew to a plaintiff wail, he rushed toward it like his boots were on fire. On the floor, curled up next to Sarge, was Lydia. Her tearstained face was buried in Sarge's fur. The poor dog looked up at him as if to say *save me*.

Wes dropped to his knees. "Hey, sweetheart." He moved her damp hair from in front of her eyes. Those beautiful swollen eyes ringed in red. With an empty wineglass next to her, Wes knew things in Lydia's life had taken a turn for the worse.

He pried her fists from Sarge's fur and pulled her to his chest. He didn't expect her to climb into his arms, but she did. He fell back to lean against the wall and lifted her onto his lap. "It's okay," he whispered against her hair. Today she didn't smell like peaches. She smelled like him, and he liked how that made him feel. Possessiveness came over him bringing out the need to protect her.

She sobbed until his shirt was soggy. "I'm sorry."

"Shh, it's okay. You have nothing to be sorry about. A good cry is sometimes the best thing." He still had no idea what happened to her. Had the asshole boyfriend reached out and twisted her wounded heart? It was hard to tell with women. For all he knew she could have eaten her last candy bar or finished a good book or recently watched a Nicholas Sparks movie. That always sent Courtney for the Kleenex, but something told Wes this anguish went deeper.

He lifted her chin and thumbed the tears from beneath her eyes. "Tell me what's wrong." Without thought, his lips brushed the top of her head.

Several jagged breaths later she leaned back and said, "My life is over."

He cupped her cheeks with both hands. "Your life isn't over."

She crumbled against him and cried more. Between the hiccups and whimpers that nearly broke his heart, he held her tight and asked her to explain.

"I've let them all down. My parents. My grandparents. When they died, I promised them I'd become something. Their expectations of me shouldn't end because their lives did. I wanted to become someone they could be proud of. Today I got the final rejection letter. I'll never be anything." Her cries grew louder while his hug grew tighter. "No one wants to hire me. No one wants me."

Wes waited until her sobbing stopped before he stood and put her into a chair at the table. A quick refill of her wineglass and a cold beer for him and he was back at her side.

"That's not true."

She laughed, not the funny laugh that came from humor, but the kind that came from hysteria.

"But it is. You think Adam was the first to bail on me. Hell, the longest relationship I've ever had is with my sister, and that's because I'm like a sticky booger she can't shake off. How sad is that?"

All he wanted was to pick her up and set her back on his lap. Instead, he brought the cold beer to his lips. It was the only thing stopping him from kissing hers. Showing her how wrong she was. He wanted her. "If other men don't see your value, you're not looking at the right men."

Lydia's head bobbled like a dashboard toy. "Men are like puppies, they're adorable when you take them home but then they crap all over everything."

Wes pointed to his chest. "Man here. Although a lot of men are assholes, some of us aren't."

She looked shocked as if she only just realized he was there. "God, I'm the puppy in this situation. You've done everything to help me, and I just crapped all over your gender. I'm sorry."

She reached out and laid her hand on his knee. The heat of her touch raced straight to his groin. How long had it been since he made love to a woman? He pressed his memory for a face—a name—a time. All he could come up with was the vague memory of a girl in Vail the weekend of his divorce. That was nearly a year ago. No wonder Lydia's touch made him hard as stone. He'd gone far too long without, but after the failure of his marriage, he promised himself to not get involved with a woman who didn't want what he did. His relationship with Courtney had been like blending oil and water. Outside of the bedroom, they'd never truly come together.

"I get you're unhappy. Maybe you need to revisit your

goals and choices. Maybe this is the universe telling you to take a step back and evaluate."

"All right, all wise and powerful one, next you'll be telling me to take my lemons and make lemonade."

"Only if you like lemonade. If not, make something else."

"Not much use for lemons." She dipped her finger into her wine and rimmed the glass until a note rang out. Sarge ran into the kitchen and howled at the pitch. Lydia laughed, which was a far better sight than her tears.

"Go get changed. You're full of dog hair. It's karaoke night at Bishop's Brewhouse and you're going. It's an unwritten town requirement to show."

She tipped back her glass and gulped down her wine. "I've been told, but I don't really feel like being around happy people. Makes it more clear how miserable I am."

He set his beer down. "What you need is an attitude adjustment." He bent over and gently picked her up. When she squirmed, he tossed her over his shoulder. One hand wrapped around her thighs while the other pressed against her ass. He knew it would feel perfect under his touch.

"What are you doing?"

"Taking control." He marched down the hallway, up the stairs, and set her on her feet in front of the door. "Get changed. I'm going to shower and dress, and then I'm taking you out and you will have fun."

"You can't make me have fun." She blew the hair that had fallen in front of her face away. He loved the way she puckered her lips and fisted her hips to get her way. It might have worked in the past with other men. Not tonight. Not with him.

"Is that a challenge? I love a challenge. Be ready in twenty minutes, or I'll strip you down and change you myself." He left her standing in the hallway. The heat of her stare warmed him through and through.

In the bathroom, he tugged his bandage loose. The stitches weren't irritated or swollen. In fact, his hand only hurt if he pressed firmly against the wound.

Stripped down, he entered the shower and let the jets work their magic on his tense muscles while his good hand worked out the strain between his legs. He closed his eyes and his imagination conjured up the perfect woman. The only problem was she looked a hell of a lot like Lydia. Only this girl's eyes smiled when she did. Wes decided on his new mission. If he could turn an old house into a masterpiece, why couldn't he make a miserable woman happy?

Standing in front of the mirror with only a towel wrapped around his waist, he heard a light tap coming from her door.

"Are you decent?"

He looked down at the towel. "Depends on what you'd call decent, but you can come in. I'm not showing anything you haven't seen already."

The door opened slowly. Lydia entered the bathroom wearing a short flowery skirt and a white shirt that covered nothing but her boobs. On her feet was a pair of sandals.

"Hell, I'm wearing more than you." Wes took her in. He didn't think it was possible for her to be any sexier than she was in her nightshirt and boxer shorts. Shorts he hoped didn't belong to that asshole Adam. Standing in front of him was Lydia the woman, and she put Lydia the doctor to shame.

"Too much?"

"You want to wear less?" The twitch between his legs made him press his body against the cold edge of the sink. The last thing he needed was to embarrass himself further by standing in front of her like a teenage boy after seeing his first girly magazine.

"I mean, is this not appropriate?"

The uncertainty in her eyes broke him. "You look perfect, Lydia. Sexy as hell."

When she blushed and smiled, a little sparkle lit up her eyes. "Thank you." She walked forward and leaned her head against his chest. The natural thing for him to do was hug her. Having her in his arms spurred on the next natural reaction, which no doubt she felt pressed against her stomach, but it was too late. What was done was done.

When her hands rested on his chest, the moment was perfect until he remembered this wasn't real. Unless Lydia did a full one-hundred-and-eighty-degree turn, she could never be his. Her options might be limited, but she kept one foot facing each direction, waiting to sprint to the side that offered the best deal. The scales weren't tipped in his favor, but he'd work on that. Maybe she'd see everything she could want or need was right here in Aspen Cove.

"I'm going to get dressed while you do whatever it is you think you need to do in here. I'll tell you you're perfect the way you are."

She stepped away and looked at his tented towel. "You're perfect too."

He wanted to laugh because compared to her last three-inch asshole, Wes had so much more to offer.

He beat her downstairs. Since he'd promised Sarge a trip to the bar, Wes leashed him up and loaded him into the truck. When he got back to the house, Lydia was waiting in the kitchen. Her hair shone like spun gold. Her eyes popped with a little sparkly shadow and long black lashes, but it was her shiny ripe red lips that got him. When she flicked her tongue out to taste the gloss, he got jealous.

"What flavor is that?"

She ringed her lips with her tongue. "Watermelon. Samantha gave each of us girls a tube the last time I was here."

Wes wet his lips. Even though he couldn't taste it, he could imagine how sweet a kiss from Lydia would be. If he didn't get her in the truck and on the road, he knew he'd do just about anything to get a taste.

"Ready?"

She lifted her shoulders. "As ready as I'll ever be."

Minutes later, he parked the truck in front of Bishop's Brewhouse and raced around to let Lydia out. Sarge jumped across her lap and took off for the door. "Sorry about that. It's hard to control him when he knows what he wants. He's got a soft spot for your sister's dog."

"Otis has a way with everyone. He's friends with the cat. You can't account for taste."

"It's strange how happiness is found in the unlikeliest of places with unexpected companions."

"Yeah, yeah, are we talking lemons again?"

"No, we're talking lemonade. Let's go, beautiful. The world awaits your greatness."

He opened the door for her and entered the already full bar. In the corner was one empty stool. Wes rushed forward to save it for Lydia.

"Have a seat. What would you like?" Cannon walked over with a stout and a glass of white wine.

"Look, I'm already a regular." She held up her glass and tapped his mug. "Here's to hot men in bath towels." When she winked, a warm heat washed over him.

"Any particular man in a towel you're referring too?"

She looked around the bar which had men outnumbering women three to one. "Keeping my options open."

"The odds are in your favor."

"It would seem, but honestly the odds never fall in my favor."

"Today is the first day of the rest of your life. Make different choices and see what happens."

Sheriff Cooper tapped the mic. "Drink responsibly and don't drive intoxicated."

Everyone lifted their drinks to toast. One of the new guys said he'd only drink until he was influenced.

"I'll be seeing you later," the sheriff said. "I've got a room ready."

Karaoke started with Katie, who arrived with a tray of leftover muffins that were devoured in seconds.

She handed the mic to Bayden Lockhart, who'd showed up only minutes before with his brothers.

"Now that would have been my type," Lydia said.

"Bayden?"

"Is that Mr. Dark and Dangerous's name?"

"Yep." Wes didn't like that she had a type. Liked it less because it was opposite of him. Couldn't figure out why it mattered to him. "You met him last night with his brothers."

She leaned against the bar with her elbows back, her breasts jutted forward. He wasn't the only one to notice.

"He looked familiar but I couldn't place him."

A smile broke free. Bayden might be her type, but he wasn't memorable. He sang a song and passed the mic to someone else. The night went by quickly. By nine o'clock only the jukebox sang.

A few brave men approached Lydia and asked her to dance. Blind was more like it because the ones who caught Wes's glare turned and walked away. She took to the tiny dance floor a few times, but her eyes found his no matter where she was or who she was with.

On her fourth glass of wine she wasn't exactly stable on her feet. When some guy asked her to dance, she followed him. All the while she looked over her shoulder to Wes. He wasn't much of a dancer but when the asshole cupped her ass and wouldn't let her get away, he rushed to her side. "You need to drop your hand, asshole, or you'll lose it, and she's the only qualified physician capable of reattaching it."

The guy raised his hand in surrender and stepped away. "Didn't know she was taken. She said yes."

"To the dance, not to pawing her to death." Wes pulled Lydia to his chest and swayed to the music.

"I thought you'd never dance with me."

"Is that what you wanted?" His hands rested on her hips.

Her cheek pressed to his chest. Could she hear the way his heart raced?

"I thought it would be nice." Air whooshed from her in a contented sigh.

"You'll never get what you want if you don't ask for it."

"What if I wanted to kiss you?" She stared up at him with desire in her eyes.

He pressed his lips to her forehead. "I'd tell you to wait until you were sober and then ask me."

"Figures." She stepped away.

"Is this where you get mad at me again and tell me I'm not cute?" The music ended, and he walked her back to the bar where Cannon had another glass of wine waiting. Since Wes was the designated driver, she could drink as much as she wanted. He'd switched to water two hours ago.

"No, this is where I tell you thank you for being such a stand-up guy right before I tell you what an idiot you are to not take me up on my offer. I'm a damn good kisser."

She reached across the bar and tugged on her sister's sleeve. "Tell him I'm a good kisser."

Sage's eyes shot wide. "Someone's had enough wine." She mouthed the word, "Sorry."

"Tell him," Lydia begged.

"I can't say firsthand, but she's a Nichols and we have lips that taste like honey." She tapped Cannon. "Isn't that right, sweetheart?"

Cannon turned around. "Isn't what right?"

Sage lifted on tiptoes and kissed him. "Just agree, baby, it's the safest response."

"Anything Sage says is true," he replied.

"Smart man," Wes tossed back. "I think it's time I got your sister back to the house."

Lydia had gulped down her wine and laid her head on the bar.

"Are you sure you can handle her? I can take her to our place. We've got a couch with her name on it." The concern in Sage's eyes was obvious. She loved her sister without reservation.

"No, I'll take her home and put her in my bed."

Cannon and Sage looked at him.

"See," Lydia slurred. "He'll take me to bed, but won't give me a kiss."

"I meant I'll take her to her room and put her to sleep. She'll be fine." Lord, how he wished the other scenario was true, but if Lydia ever made it to his bed it would be when she was sober.

"Let me take you home." He guided her outside. Sarge followed behind. She stumbled a few times on her way to the truck, but she got there intact.

During the short drive home, she fell asleep.

In his arms, he carried her upstairs and placed her on

top of the bed covers. Her eyes fluttered open when he removed her shoes and pulled the covers from beneath her body.

"I really wanted you to kiss me," she murmured.

He sat on the edge of her bed and tugged the comforter over her body. "You want to know a secret?"

She leaned forward and nodded.

"I really wanted to kiss you too." He pressed his lips to hers in a gentle chaste kiss. "Love that watermelon."

She was asleep before he closed the door.

CHAPTER ELEVEN

"Oh Lord." A sliver of light filtered through the blinds and poked Lydia straight in the eye. She covered her face and groaned. Next to her the furry beast stretched and kicked, nearly pushing her off the bed. If waking up with a bass drum beating inside her head and a seventy-pound canine beating her body wasn't bad enough, her mouth had traversed the desert all night. Cottonmouth didn't begin to describe the arid landscape of her tongue.

Tossing off the blanket revealed she'd slept in her clothes. The same clothes she'd worn to the bar. The pounding in her head increased when she sat up and looked around. On the nightstand was a glass of water and two painkillers.

Her heart beat in time with the percussion thumping inside her brain. *What the hell did I do?* The small tablets stuck to her tongue until the rush of water washed them down.

Oh hell. Lydia knew wine was the worst panacea for disappointment. The artificial high never lasted long enough to get through the reality of the low. She slipped off the bed onto her bare feet and walked past her sandals sitting neatly against the wall.

Between the painful beats she tried to get a clear picture of last night. There had been the message, the wine, the bar and Wes. He'd danced with her once.

She walked into the steamy bathroom and stood in front of the sink. With the hand towel she found on the counter, she wiped the fog from the mirror and groaned. After a splash of cold water she realized all was not right in her world.

In the mirror's reflection was a very naked Wes leaning against the shower wall as the jets massaged his body. The right thing to do would be to turn around and leave, but that was not what she did. She watched him through the foggy veil floating around his body. Broad shoulders angled to narrow hips that ended at an ass carved by the gods. Perfect stonelike globes led to strong thighs that could no doubt crack coconuts with a single squeeze.

Wes Covington was a sight to behold. He was a construction worker fantasy come to life. It got better when he turned and Lydia got a glimpse of his hammer. Heavy and thick in his hand, she knew without a doubt he'd be able to hit all the right spots with his tool.

When her eyes slid up his body, she found him looking at her.

"See something interesting?"

Oh God. She was caught in the act. It was bad enough to get drunk and be put to bed last night but getting caught looking at him was too much. All she wanted to do was melt into the floorboards.

Lydia took another long look before she straightened her shoulders and put a mask of indifference on her face.

"Basic equipment. Anatomy 101." She turned around

and faced the mirror as if it was a normal occurrence to have a sexy, naked man showering behind her. She reached for her toothbrush while he stepped out of the shower and stretched for a towel.

The mist circled his body like a blanket. Water droplets dripped to the tile floor. With inches separating them, he leaned in and said, "Oh, sweetheart, if you think this is basic equipment you need a refresher course." He wrapped the towel over his shoulders, leaving his body exposed. Wes didn't have an ounce of self-consciousness. Then again, with a body like Zeus and a hammer like Thor, what was there to hide?

"Have you no shame?" Lydia stood back. No matter how hard she tried to not look, she took him in like a cat watching a mouse.

"What's there to be ashamed of? I'm not the voyeur."

That was the indisputable truth. She was the trespasser. The creeper peeper. The shower stalker. After one last glance at his perfection, she turned on the water and put a line of toothpaste on her brush.

"Sorry, I didn't hear or see you showering. All I could hear when I entered was the drum line in my head. All I saw was the need to brush my teeth."

Wes chuckled. "That's not all you saw." He looked down at his heavy, hanging length.

Damn the man for making her look again. "What the hell am I doing?" She set her readied toothbrush on the sink and turned toward her room. "I'll come back when the bathroom isn't occupied." She wanted to look over her shoulder but didn't for fear her feet would be glued to the floor and her eyes stuck on him.

"You don't have to leave, Lydia, we're grown-ups. Surely we can share a bathroom."

It took everything in her to walk into her room and close the door. Somehow the ache in her head had descended to the space between her thighs. She wasn't sure which was more painful.

She climbed back into bed and waited for a sign that Wes had finished in the bathroom. She knew as soon as Sarge leaped from the bed it was safe for her to enter.

The fog had lifted, and the mirror cleared. Staring back at her were dark baggy eyes, bedhead, and a sallow complexion. It was a wonder that Wes hadn't seen her and run from the bathroom. She looked at the connecting door and almost locked it but didn't. Wes would probably never enter but a thrill raced through her knowing he could.

Thirty minutes later she walked down the stairs to the kitchen, where he sat at the table talking on the phone.

"Glad it's going great."

Lydia heard only his side of the conversation, but his voice was pleasant and positive.

"No need to come by. Enjoy the visit with your parents."

At the coffeepot, she poured herself a mug and turned around to see Wes staring at her. He lifted a Pop-Tart and pointed to the cupboard.

There were worse things to put in her body. The most recent that came to mind was wine. Last night was a blur. She walked to the cabinet she'd alphabetized and worked her way to the shelf that held P items. Maybe she should have shelved them by flavor.

She plopped two cinnamon tarts into the toaster and leaned against the counter.

"Unnecessary. Really, stay in Vail. I won't be around, anyway. We have the grand opening of the park today." Wes sipped his coffee. "Yep, talk to you later." He set his phone down and looked at her. "Feeling better? How's that ache?"

"What?" No way could he be talking about the throbbing in her core.

The toaster buzzed and the Pop-Tarts rose. She pinched one between her fingers and lifted it to a waiting plate.

"Your headache?"

"Oh, it's getting better." How was it she'd just seen the man naked, and he was sitting at the table as if nothing happened? *Nothing happened.* "Did you put me into bed last night?"

A sly smile lifted the corners of his lush lips. "I did. You don't remember?"

A feeling of dread seeped deep into her bones. She was fairly bold when she was sober. Give her a drink or two and she had no filter or fear.

She pulled her lower lip between her teeth. Gnawed on it until it turned numb. "I've got nothin'." She really had no recollection past... *Oh shit. I asked him to kiss me.* "Oh boy. I may have asked you to kiss me. Was that a dream?"

Wes rose from his seat and walked to the coffeepot for a refill before he returned, which meant he was staying longer. Hard enough to get through what she did this morning and now she had to relive last night.

"I've got no idea what you dreamed, but I'd love to be inside your head and watch."

She picked up the pastry and nibbled around the edges. It was a habit of hers to eat the outside crust before the filling. Sometimes you had to make it through the less exciting stuff to get to the good parts. The problem with this situation was she remembered none of the parts.

"You didn't answer the question?"

"Did I kiss you?"

She let out a frustrated breath. "Yes, Wes, did you kiss me?"

He appeared to enjoy her discomfort. "Well, as a matter of fact, I did."

Ba boom, ba boom, ba boom her heart raced until it became *boom boom boom boom.*

She dropped her breakfast to the plate and buried her face in her hands. "I'm so embarrassed."

"Nothing to be embarrassed about."

The heat of her blush burned her cheeks. She licked her lips, hoping that action would spur a memory. As if she'd taste him. There was nothing. Mad at herself for her lack of control, she lashed out. "Couldn't have been a good kiss if I don't remember it."

"Below par as far as kisses go. You want a memorable kiss, all you have to do is ask." He reached for the bag of bandages and pulled out the gauze and tape. "Give me a hand?"

"You insult my kisses and now you want help?" Surely the kiss couldn't have been that bad. How bad could her kiss be?

He moved his hand to the center of the table palm up. "I didn't insult your kiss."

She tugged his hand and wrapped the wound with gauze. She might have tugged it a little too tight. Certain she did when he hissed. As much as she wanted him to suffer for his comment, she couldn't in her right mind torture him, so she loosened the bandage and taped it in place. "You don't think calling our first kiss subpar is an insult?"

Wes's laugh filled the air. Even Sarge lifted his head to see what was going on. "Lydia, you asked me to kiss you several times. I refused. Not because I don't find you attractive. I think you're stunning."

"Why did you give in and kiss me?"

He moved his chair so he sat next to her. When he twisted his body, they were close enough for a repeat performance.

"Against my better judgment, I gave in because I couldn't resist." He lifted his shoulders and let them drop.

She watched his lips as he spoke—full, lush lips that surely gave memorable kisses. She hated that she couldn't recall the moment. "Sorry I disappointed you." Her shoulders tipped forward and her head hung low.

Wes thumbed her chin up, forcing her to look at him. "Lydia, you weren't a disappointment. We barely brushed lips and honestly you were already passed out when that happened. I told you last night if you really wanted a kiss you needed to ask me for it when you were sober."

His words worked their way from her head to her heart. "You didn't want to take advantage of me." The words came out in soft awe because so many people would have taken what she'd drunkenly offered.

"I'm not that guy." He let go of her chin and cupped her cheek. "I hear you're an amazing kisser, Lydia."

She smiled. "Who told you?"

He leaned forward. "You did," he whispered across her lips.

"I could do better." She shifted her body so her knees moved between his thighs. Face to face, their lips were a separated by a breath. "I want to do better."

"Overachiever?" The hand that had cupped her cheek now cradled her neck.

He was close enough for her to see the gemstone flecks in his eyes. When she inhaled, she breathed in the citrus and spice that mixed with his scent. Lust and need made her dizzy. Her head spun. Unsteady, she palmed his chest for balance. The hard muscle flexed under her hand. Her fingers trailed down his chest to explore every hill and valley of sinew.

She breathed deeply. "Call it what you want, but kiss me."

Soft and sure, his lips pressed to hers. It wasn't a frenzied kiss, but a measured moment until she parted her lips to grant him access. He dipped his tongue inside and slid it across her tongue for a languid taste.

Fingers threaded through her hair, he gripped her tight and pulled her closer to deepen the kiss. Sweet like honey, his mouth moved over hers. His soft, velvet tongue danced across hers. She knew he was a busy man, but he sat there and kissed her like he had all day. When he pulled away, he nipped at her bottom lip until he sucked it into his mouth. Rockets of desire shot like fireworks through her body.

With a pop, he released her lip and sat back. His eyes burned with passion. The kind of passion she had always wanted to see from a lover but never did.

"Now that's a kiss I'll remember." He lifted from the seat and gathered his dishes. "I'll see you at the park." Then he was gone.

Lydia sat at the table in silence reliving the best kiss of her life.

CHAPTER TWELVE

"Stop looking at me like that." Sarge sat in the seat next to Wes, staring at him like he'd stolen his bone. "How was I supposed to resist when she was sitting in front of me asking for another kiss?"

Sarge turned and lay down with his tail end facing Wes.

"You get to sleep with her. All I got was a kiss."

He thought about that kiss all the way to the site. How her lips fit flush against his like they were molded for each other. How her kisses tasted like honey and cinnamon. The way her hands felt on his chest. Though he'd told himself Lydia wasn't the woman for him, that kiss made him a liar. She was perfect. All he had to do was convince her to stay.

Four black pickups sat in front of the old mill, their doors emblazoned with the Lockhart logo—a heart-shaped lock. It was clever branding for their name. Too bad Wes was saddled with Covington. There was no easy way to advertise his brand. His logo was Covington Construction on top of a horizontal ladder. It was simple, but it worked.

Sarge hopped out of the truck after him and wandered into the open door.

Wes wanted to see how much the Lockharts finished yesterday. They had to gut the place before the renovation could start. When he entered he was surprised at how much had been accomplished.

Noah lifted his head. "Hey, man. How's things?" He took off his glove and held out his hand.

Wes liked a good firm handshake. It was the sign of a confident man. "I can't complain." *Not after Lydia's kiss.* He knew he had to get his head clear. Hard labor would do that for sure. "Thought I'd stop by and help."

"We'll never turn down free labor." Noah led him to the center of the factory floor, where ancient machines were once used to press pulp into paper. "We're dismantling this weekend and hauling it all away on Monday."

Wes's eyes grew big. There were at least a dozen pieces of machinery to dismantle. The sheer size of them made him doubt the job could be finished by Monday, but as he scanned the warehouse, he saw the Lockhart brothers moved together like a well-oiled machine.

They put him to work loosening bolts. Noah and Ethan followed him by dismantling parts while Bayden and Quinn carried it all outside. They worked like this for several hours. When it was nearing noon he cut out to shower and get to the park. He was part of the barbecue crew.

At home, he was alone. Lydia had probably hightailed it out of the house after the kiss. Her absence made taking a shower boring. This morning, he'd noticed her the minute she came in. What really alerted him was the breeze that floated past the heat of the water to prickle his skin. He kept his back turned waiting for her to realize the bathroom was occupied.

When she didn't leave, he shifted to face her. He wasn't a nudist, but he wasn't ashamed of his body either. The way

Lydia looked at him, the hunger and interest in her eyes made it hard to cover up. He loved the way she pulled back her shoulders as if she weren't affected.

He was affected. He could have hung the towel on his pole.

Twenty minutes later, he was back in the truck with Sarge.

Parking was at a premium when he arrived at the park. A crowd lined up on the edge of the grass. In the center were the Bishops, who had funded the park. Katie had actually donated part of her trust fund to make it all happen. It had been the first big project in Aspen Cove that Wes oversaw.

The two hundred thousand dollars she'd spent was well worth it. At least a hundred kids rocked on their heels waiting for Katie to cut the ribbon. Behind her, on the perimeter of the property, were vendors from all over town. Kind of like a country fair without the rides.

There was a tap on the microphone and the air grew silent but the energy of anticipation was thick.

"I'm not much of a public speaker," Katie said. She bounced her daughter, Sahara, on her hip. "All I want to say is I'm so happy to give back to the community that gave me everything." Tears flowed from her eyes. If there was ever a perfect script for a Hallmark movie, it was Katie's story. She passed Sahara to Bowie and picked up the oversized scissors. "Everything is free today, grab an ice cream from Sam's Scoop, a hotdog or hamburger from my husband and the other good-looking men from Aspen Cove. Visit the bouncy castle. Get your face painted by Maisey and Ben. If you need first aid, go visit Sage and Lydia in the blue tent. Most of all, have fun." She cut through the ribbon and huddled against Bowie until the stampede passed by.

Wes and Sarge took it all in. The swing sets, the jungle gym, the rock-climbing wall. To the far right sat the baseball field. Sign-ups for both a children's league and an adult coed league were posted in the bakery, the diner, and the bar.

He walked the perimeter feeling proud that he had played a part in creating a place that would bring the townspeople together. It was important to him to help build the community.

"You're here." Katie lifted up on tiptoes and kissed his cheek. "Thanks for volunteering all your time."

He turned in a circle. "It's amazing."

"It wouldn't have come together without you."

He shook his head. "It takes a village."

The adults gathered under the pavilion to listen to Samantha sing. She promised a sneak peek of her new album. On each table was a fireman's boot to collect donations. Until the town grew big enough for taxes to pay for a crew, they would have to depend on donations, the largest coming from Samantha, to finance the fire department. Wes volunteered his services to build the firehouse, but Samantha insisted she pay him his normal fees for the Guild Center.

He didn't need the money. He'd inherited a sizable amount from his grandfather. He'd also tucked away a small fortune from his architectural projects. His earnings from the center would be set aside until something important came up—something that would benefit the community.

Sahara started crying. "I've got to feed her. She's as serious about her meals as Bowie. I'll catch ya later." Katie hurried off in the direction of the pavilion, while Wes gravitated toward the first aid tent.

Behind a table dressed in navy blue scrubs was Lydia. When he entered, her cheeks flushed red.

"Need a Band-Aid?"

"Nope. Just stopping by to say hello."

Sage set out flyers and pamphlets and smiley face stickers. He picked a sticker up and held it in the air. "Do I deserve one?"

Lydia's eyes grew big. She swiped the sticker from his hand. "You didn't cry when I changed your bandage so I suppose you earned it." She peeled it from the backing and pressed it to his chest. Her hand lingered there until Sage spoke.

"Hell, he had to carry you home. That alone deserves a sticker. I'm surprised you're here."

Lydia swiped her hand back and stepped away. "Not a proud moment."

"Nothing to be ashamed of," he said while his eyes held hers. "I was being neighborly. We'd hate for your time in Aspen Cove to be subpar."

Her lips parted and her jaw fell open. All he wanted to do was kiss her again, but he wouldn't until he could figure out where this thing with Lydia was headed.

Sage stepped in front of the table and stood in front of Wes. "So did you ever give my sister that kiss she begged for?"

"Oh my God," Lydia said. "You didn't just ask him that."

Sage grinned. "I owe you for all those years you picked on me. So what about that kiss?"

Wes looked between the two sisters. "A gentleman never tells." He glanced past Sage to Lydia. "I'm getting an ice cream, you want to come?"

Lydia wasted no time rounding the table. "It's ice cream or beat my sister to death. I'll take ice cream."

He rested his hand at the curve of her back and led her into the sun. The line was long at Sam's Scoops but moved fast so it didn't take them long to get to the front.

Wes was used to the colorful names Sam used for his flavors. Today's were Cherry Potter, Mintnight Madness and Rockin' Roadie.

"Cherry Potter?" Lydia stared at the menu as if waiting for the options to change.

"Just try it." Wes asked for a scoop of Cherry Potter for her and a scoop of Rockin' Roadie for him.

Sam plopped a big sloppy spoonful into each cone and sprinkled chocolate bits on top. "Got to have the chocolate-covered ants."

"Ants?" Eyes big, mouth twisted, Lydia stared at the brown specks, appalled.

He led her away from the window. "Nothing to worry about, it's chocolate-covered puffed rice."

"Oh my God, why would he do that?"

Wes laughed. "He likes to razz the kids. You haven't had anything until you've tried Unicorn Poop."

"I don't even want to know. I'll stick with my cherries with marshmallows and ants." She puckered her lips and pressed them into the pink cream. When her tongue snuck out to lick what remained, Wes wanted to help her out. He glanced around and found no one watching so he leaned in and licked the sweet cream she'd missed.

"Hey, that was mine." She bent forward and licked at his chocolate mint cone. "If you're going to sneak a taste so will I."

"You want a taste?" He tapped her lips with his scoop and moved forward to lick it off. Just as his lips touched hers, Sarge, who had been a silent shadow the whole time, let out a low menacing growl.

Wes wanted to kill the dog, but he rarely growled so something was up. When he turned around to take in the surroundings, a flash of pink barreled into him.

"Surprise!" Courtney had practically crawled up his body. "Did you miss me?" Prying her free was like peeling a skin from a banana.

He stepped back and looked at Lydia, whose face showed no emotion. She inched away from him in tiny steps. Wes turned back to his ex-wife. "I told you not to come."

"Oh, baby. I missed you. Of course I'd come. You built this park. It's a big deal."

"You built this park?" Lydia asked.

"He did," Courtney bubbled. "My Wes is so talented."

Lydia stepped farther back. "Your Wes? Who are you?"

Courtney offered her hand. "I'm Courtney Covington, his wife."

Wes watched Lydia's face turn white and her cone drop to the grass. "Ex-wife. She's my ex-wife."

Lydia's eyes narrowed. A protective mask of indifference stole her smile. "Nice to meet you. I should get back to the tent."

"Tent?"

Wes wrapped his arm around Lydia's shoulders. "Lydia is the new doctor in town."

"Oh, how sweet."

He leaned down and whispered in her ear. "She's my past, not my present."

Lydia smiled, but it didn't reach her eyes. "Funny how the past seems to haunt us all." She shrugged out of his hold and walked away.

CHAPTER THIRTEEN

"He has a damn wife?" Lydia mumbled as she entered the first aid tent.

Sage sat in a chair reading a book. Her eyes stayed on the page for a few more seconds. "Who has a wife?"

Lydia hid behind the tent flap, looking toward Wes, who stood next to Courtney. From her hiding place she could see the couple clearly. "Wes has a wife."

"No, he doesn't." She rose from her chair and pressed herself against Lydia's back.

With Sage being significantly shorter, Lydia tugged her sister in front of her and pointed to where Wes stood with the tall brunette.

"He says she's his ex-wife, but she's not acting like an ex anything."

"Why do you care?"

"I don't care." Lydia peeked out again.

"Obviously, since you're obsessed with watching him."

"Not obsessed. I'm merely curious. It's a professional interest since he's my patient." She rolled her eyes at no one.

Maybe she rolled them at herself for saying such a stupid thing.

Sage returned to the table, flopped into her chair, and dug out a bag of Skittles. "Right, because patching up his hand has everything to do with who he sees. Did you kiss him?"

"What? What does it matter?" She gripped the tent fabric and turned toward the park again. Courtney moved forward, Wes moved back. In the end, he gave her a hug and moved in Lydia's direction.

"Because you're obsessing over him. Was it a good kiss?"

Lydia gave up. "The best. Kisses like a porn star kiss. He made my toes curl and my heart leap." As he neared, she raced to the other side of the table and picked up Sage's book, opening it to the center. "Pretend everything is okay."

Sage yanked her book back. "Everything *is* okay."

Wes ducked under the tent and squinted while his eyes adjusted to the lack of light. "Sorry about that." He looked from Lydia to Sage. "Can I borrow your sister for a minute?"

Sage's brows lifted. "Borrow? No. Keep her? Absolutely."

Lydia reached over and pinched her sister's rib cage. She knew getting the tiniest bit of skin and twisting would make her scream. "Behave. I'm older and wiser than you." When Sage yelped, Lydia let go.

Sage rose and stepped away, no doubt getting out of reach. "Older? Yes. Wiser? No damn way." She swiped her bag of Skittles from the table and exited the tent, leaving Lydia and Wes alone.

"Can I sit down?" He nodded toward the empty seat beside her.

"Sure. Something you needed?" Her attempt to sound

indifferent failed. It was hard to pull off when Wes was so close. So tempting. So damn sexy.

"I wanted to explain." His fingers slipped under the seat to drag it closer before he sat down.

"You don't owe me an explanation." He was too close. His presence made her skin tingle or maybe he made her itch. Was that the issue? He was bad for her and her body knew it before her brain. Like an allergic reaction?

He palmed her knee, and a charge of heat skittered up her thigh and landed in her core. Molten lava rushed through her veins, the pulse of an eruption throbbing just below the surface. "I saw your face. I'm not Adam."

She couldn't help herself. The mention of Adam had her eyes skimming his body and landing at his zipper. A silly giggle burst forth. "No, you are definitely not Adam." She held her hands out roughly three inches apart and expanded the space to eight.

Wes covered her hands and expanded it by an inch. "If we're going to be transparent, we should use facts." His chuckle warmed her heart.

"What are the facts?" She rested her hands on her thighs. His fell to his side.

"Courtney was a bad decision made in haste. We got along and enjoyed each other. We married impetuously." He winked. "Another big word."

"Seriously? Aren't we over that?"

Wes shook his head. "I'm going to milk that for all it's worth."

"Whatever. Go on, Mr. I'm a Simple Man with a Killer Vocabulary."

"Not much more to say. We had different goals. She wanted a law degree and big city living. I'm not interested in that."

"I'd say you communicated poorly?" Wasn't that the problem she had with Adam? Their issues went beyond lack of communication. Hell, they lacked everything.

"I'd have to agree." He leaned back in the chair and stretched his long legs in front of him.

Lydia had a hard time concentrating. She'd seen him naked. Even though he was fully clothed, she still saw him nude in her mind.

"Seems to be an epidemic with relationships." Lydia looked to the opening of the tent. "Courtney doesn't seem like she's received the message you two are divorced."

He rocked his head from side to side. "She's a friend. She's a good woman. She's just not my woman."

Lydia let that soak in for a minute. "What if she had stayed here? Would you still love her?"

Wes leaned forward, only inches from her face. "I'm not sure love was ever a part of the equation. I'm not going to kiss and tell. It's not my style. All I can say is she never lived here. We lived in Denver when we were married. It was a short union, and she moved to Boston."

Lydia rubbed her face in her hands. "So she was great in bed." When she looked at Wes, she saw nothing in his expression. He'd masked it because that was the man he was. He wouldn't tell her sister they'd kissed, and he wouldn't tell Lydia that somehow Courtney had a magical vagina. "She called you *her Wes*. I don't think she's finished with you yet."

"Are you jealous?"

Was she? The answer was yes, but she had no reason to be. Wes wasn't hers. She had no plans to stay in Aspen Cove. Anything that happened between them would be superficial and short-lived.

"No, of course not. I have no claim to you."

"We kissed." He shifted forward so they touched foreheads. "It was a great kiss."

There was no hope for her. She needed to know. "Better than kissing Courtney?" She drew back and lifted a brow.

Wes narrowed his eyes. "Still trying to get me to talk, are you?"

"A girl has to know her strengths."

He leaned back and smiled. "Kissing is one of yours."

Happiness bubbled inside her. The effervescent feeling brought a smile to her face.

"I love it when your smile reaches your eyes. They almost change color. Go from steely gray to sunny sky blue. Beautiful."

"How the hell are you single?" Lydia couldn't imagine how Courtney could have wanted something more than Wes.

"Interesting question coming from the woman who alphabetized my dry goods and did my laundry. I have my faults."

"Being sloppy and disorganized aren't deal breakers. Those are bad habits, not character flaws. You can correct a habit, while with a character flaw you're stuck."

"I don't know what that asshole did to you outside of what you told me, but he let a good thing go."

"Thank you for seeing good in me. Even if it's only my kissing skills."

Wes laughed. "Let's not forget your OCD, that's been beneficial to me. Let's talk about your lack of respect for personal space."

She tried to suppress a smile. "Oh you mean the show you gave me in the bathroom? To leave would have been disrespectful," she teased.

"To stay can get you in trouble." He leaned in and

brushed his lips across hers. "Might get me in trouble. I'm not looking for trouble."

God she wanted a little trouble. Needed a little trouble if it came packaged as Wes. Grandma Dotty always said the best way to get over one man was to get under another.

"What are you looking for?"

"Forever."

That answer deflated her like a popped balloon. She'd never be his forever. She had no business pretending she could be.

She stood up and walked around the table. Gaining distance was important considering she couldn't think when he was near.

"I imagine you should stop kissing me then. I'll never be your forever. I'd be another Courtney. But if you change your mind and want a here-for-now girl, I'd be interested."

Wes stood and walked up to her. He wrapped his arms around her and tugged her to his chest. "Thanks for being honest. I can't tell you what to wish for in life, but I can tell you that sometimes you get what you want in the unlikeliest of places. Wealth can be measured in more ways than money. Success doesn't need a title." He brushed his lips against her forehead and walked out of the tent.

Lydia went back to her chair, but she didn't have much time to think about his words because Bailey Brown came in crying.

Lydia lifted her to the portable exam table. "What's wrong, little one?"

Mrs. Brown huffed. "She got stung by a bee."

A chill raced through Lydia. "Show me where?"

The little girl lifted her leg and pointed to a red spot on her plump thigh.

"I tried to pull it out, but it only made it worse," Mrs.

Brown swiped at the tears under Bailey's cheeks. "Stop your crying, it's over now."

Something inside Lydia reared up like a cobra ready to strike. "It's far from over, Mrs. Brown. She has a stinger leaking venom into her leg. Have you ever been stung?" Lydia squirted hand sanitizer on her palms and rubbed them together before she gloved up.

"No. I haven't been stung, but it's not the end of the world."

Heat surged through her. "Have you ever been burned?"

Mrs. Brown stared at her daughter's bee sting while Lydia scraped at the stinger with a blunt instrument while Bailey cried.

"Yes."

"Hurt bad, right? Imagine that heat coursing through your body. That's how this feels." When the stinger popped free, Lydia pressed a piece of white medical tape to it and showed Bailey. "It all gone, sweetie." She cleaned off the area and covered it with a Band-Aid. After she tossed her gloves, she reached for the smiley face stickers and handed Bailey the whole pack. "Bee stings are the worst. You deserve extras."

Bailey wiped her tears and smiled.

"Sounds like you have experience with stings."

Lydia expected Cassidy Brown to push back since she'd basically handed her her ass over her lack of empathy toward her daughter, but instead she smiled.

"I'm allergic to them. For me it's a life-or-death matter."

Cassidy's eyes got big. She looked down at the swollen spot on Bailey's leg. "Will she be okay?"

Lydia patted Cassidy's back. "She's a tough little

monkey, this one. The swelling should go down in a few hours. If it doesn't, call the clinic."

"Thank you, Dr. Nichols. I really appreciate you taking care of Bailey."

When she looked back at the little girl, she was covered in smiley face stickers. Lydia helped her off the table. "Don't forget, those don't go up your nose."

Bailey laughed. "No silly, only fingers and Kleenex belong in your nose." She looked to her mom for approval.

Cassidy sighed, "One step at a time."

Sage walked in with two plates of burgers as the Browns walked out. "So, did you and Wes make up?"

"There is no me and Wes, but yes, he cleared it all up. He married her for sex."

Sage choked on her first bite. "He did not say that."

Lydia's shoulder shook. "No, but I read between the lines. They're friends now."

"He must be a great guy. Few couples can be friends after a breakup."

"He is a great guy, just not my guy. He wants a forever. I'm leaving." She opened the burger to find it doctored exactly the way she liked it. Sage knew what she wanted. Maybe Wes was right, knowing someone well had benefits.

"You're older but far from wiser." Sage marched behind the table. "Who are you trying to prove something to? Adam? Our dead parents? Grandma? You're a success. One of the best damn doctors I know, but you're not the brightest. Maybe it's time for a self-examination to find out what you really want."

"I know what I want."

"Fine, but while you're working eighteen hours a day and going home alone, don't call me when you're lonely. I'll be too busy telling my family how successful their aunt is."

"That was a shitty thing to say." Ten years ago Lydia would have yanked her sister's red curls and taken her to the ground. If her head didn't still ache from too much wine, she would have.

"It was, but sometimes the truth hurts. I'm not saying Wes is your guy, but you'll never have a man if you don't find a balance in your life. All work and no play makes Lydia a bitch."

They moved to opposite sides of the tent and ate in silence. If not for the few cuts and scrapes they treated, neither of them would have spoken a word.

When Bowie arrived to dismantle the first aid station, all Lydia could think about was a glass of wine. One glass to ease the tension.

CHAPTER FOURTEEN

Disappointment weighed him down. It wasn't as if Wes was searching for the perfect woman to share his life, but when perfect showed up, his hopes were buoyed. Lydia was perfect. Hotter than hell with a spitfire personality, she fascinated him. Add to that the intelligence of Einstein, and lips that tasted of honey, and he thought he'd won the lottery.

The problem was Lydia had dreams, and those dreams didn't include Aspen Cove or him.

Instead of sticking around the park where the woman he didn't want to kiss hung all over him and the one he did hid in a tent, he headed back to the work site. Side by side he labored with the Lockharts until half the machinery was dismantled and moved. When five o'clock rolled around, he invited them to Bishop's Brewhouse for a beer.

The little bar was bustling when they arrived. Not a surprise since the entire population of Aspen Cove seemed to be present.

Cannon slid a stout across the bar and glanced at the Lockhart brothers. "What can I get ya?"

They asked for lagers so Cannon took four frosted mugs from the cooler and pulled a pitcher. "Cheaper this way."

Wes lifted his hand. "It's on me."

He hadn't noticed Courtney at the bar until she sidled up next to him. "You buying?" She clung to him like lint to tape.

"Why not? I pay everything else for you."

Noah elbowed him. "You gonna introduce us?" He eyed Courtney like she was barbecued meat and he was sauce.

"Sure." He pointed to each person. "Noah. Ethan. Bayden. Quinn." Then he pointed to Courtney. "This is Courtney, my—"

"Friend," she finished. She stepped forward and stood in front of Bayden. He seemed to be a female favorite. Turns out he was lots of women's type. Considering he was over six feet tall, muscles like a superhero, and the face of a model, it made sense.

"Pool?" he asked the unoccupied brothers.

They walked over to the felt and racked the balls. Bayden thankfully stayed with Courtney.

"Damn, you get the hot ones," Noah said. "First the doc and now the model?"

Wes laughed. "It's a curse."

"Seriously," Ethan added, "how the hell do you find the only two single women within a twenty-mile radius?"

Wes nodded toward Courtney. "That one is my ex and lives in Boston. She's in the state visiting her parents and crashed the ribbon cutting party. As for the doc?" Wes looked around the crowded bar and found Lydia at the end sipping a glass of white wine. She stared back at him as if she knew he was talking about her. "Like she told you at the house, she's temporary."

"Best kind."

Unless you want more. "How about you? You got a girl?"

Noah laughed. "Hell no. Why stop at one when you can have them all?"

Wes remembered those days. Long nights. Lots of women. "How old are you?"

"Thirty-six," Noah answered.

"Thirty-four," Ethan said. He pointed to Quinn and Bayden. "The twins are thirty-two."

"Twins?" He glanced at the two brothers, who were like night and day. One had sandy-colored hair, the other almost black like the night. "Would have never guessed it."

"Not identical. Just shared the same room. Haven't been able to share anything since," Noah said. "You care if he's hitting on your ex?"

Wes leaned against the pool table. *Did he?* He didn't have to wait around to find out. Bayden leaned into Courtney and brushed his lips along her jaw line. She giggled, then turned to Wes to see if he was watching. He imagined he should have felt something, but he didn't. Instead of a flood of jealousy or a pang of possessiveness, all he felt was relief. If she was glued to a Lockhart, she wouldn't be glued to him.

"She's a big girl and can decide for herself." When she wrapped her arms around Bayden's neck and kissed him, Wes felt nothing.

But when he saw a tourist walk up to Lydia and lean in to speak to her over the noise, his blood boiled. He gripped the cue like a weapon and took a step forward.

Noah moved in front of him. "Step it back. You don't want to ruin a good day with a stupid action."

Wes's grip loosened on the cue. "You're right, but I

don't want anyone messing with her. She's had a tough year."

"Is that the only reason?" Noah looked over his shoulder toward Lydia. "I'd say you like her."

"I do, but it doesn't matter. She's set on leaving."

Noah filled his mug while Quinn racked the balls. "Make her want to stay."

"How do I do that when she has each foot pointed in two different directions?"

"Put yourself in front of one foot." He took the spot next to Wes, and they both stared at Lydia, who ignored the man and turned back to the bar and her wine.

"I'm not looking for here today, gone tomorrow. I want long-term."

"Man, long term starts one day a time."

Funny how a man who wanted one and done gave him the wisest long-term advice. There was no future with Lydia if he couldn't make her see the value of each day. He'd wheedle his way past her resistance and make her see how much Aspen Cove offered. Hell, how much he offered.

An hour later, Lydia hugged her sister and left the bar. Two hours later he finished his game with the Lockharts. Courtney had moved on to another man. When Wes noticed she was unsteady on her feet, he walked over to her.

"Be safe. Don't drink and drive."

She gave him an exaggerated eye roll. "Oh please, don't pretend like you care."

"We're not together, but it doesn't mean I don't care. I may not love you, but I don't want to see you hurt."

She smiled. "So you care. I'm touched."

"Don't turn it into more than it is. Be safe." Wes settled his tab and asked Cannon to make sure Courtney got someplace safe. Once he was certain she'd be taken care of, he headed home.

Sarge beat him to the door. As soon as it opened, he raced into the living room and jumped into Lydia's lap.

Wes heard the air rush from her lungs with an *ooompf.* "Jeez, sorry about that. The dog has lost his mind around you."

She wrapped her arms around Sarge's neck and buried her face in his fur. When she pulled back, she said, "We sleep together. That builds a connection fast."

Wes let that soak in. Maybe his thought process was wrong. Maybe here-for-now might lead to long-term.

"Lucky damn dog." He turned to see what was on the television. What he saw surprised him. "Never took you for a thriller lover."

She pushed Sarge off her lap and curled into the corner of the sofa. "I love things that make my heart race. Maybe it's why I love emergency medicine. I'm an adrenaline junkie."

He tucked that bit of information into his back pocket. "Care if I join you? I'll make popcorn."

"You don't have any." Her lower lip stuck out in a pout.

"You haven't found my stash."

She perked up. "You have a stash?"

He offered her his hand and pulled her to her feet. "Follow me. I'll hook you up."

They entered the kitchen with Sarge on their heels. He went straight for the kibble while Wes pulled a Jiffy Pop from the freezer. "It stays fresh if you freeze it."

"Jiffy Pop? No microwave popcorn?"

He shook his head and raised the tin pan. "You haven't had anything until you've had Jiffy Pop." He turned on the stovetop and placed the pan over the heat.

Lydia tried twice to hop onto the counter, but she couldn't lift herself, so Wes gripped her hips and set her on the granite next to him.

"You smell like peaches again."

"Katie got Bowie to go in and get my stuff from the bathroom. They said Abby is coming home next week so I should be able to get back to my place soon."

That bit of information meant Wes had to work fast. Having Lydia in his house was perfect. The moment she moved out, things would become impossible. He couldn't very well stand in her path if he couldn't get in the same room with her.

He brushed by her, leaned into her and over her while the popcorn cooked. It was perfect when he needed the salt from the cupboard above her head. Instead of ducking, she leaned into him and he absorbed her weight. He spent way too much time looking for the salt shaker that sat in front of him, but he liked the way she felt against his body.

She wasn't unaffected, if the increased rate of her breathing was any sign. When he pulled the popcorn from the stovetop and broke open the tinfoil tent, she breathed in deeply, but he was positive it wasn't the scent of the popcorn she inhaled since her nose was in the crook of his neck.

When she pulled back, he watched her wet her lips. She leaned in as if she'd steal a kiss and that was when he helped her down. He loved the sigh she released as she followed him into the living room and took her end of the couch.

He sat at the opposite end with the popcorn in his lap.

"Are you going to share any of that?" She picked up the remote and pressed play.

"Slide closer and you can have all that you want." He patted the leather cushion next to him.

She inched over and dipped her fingers inside for a hot buttery bite.

The hum of satisfaction made him hard, so he set the container on top of his length to hide his arousal. She moved closer and closer until her head leaned against his arm. *This is perfect.*

Thirty minutes from the end of the movie, Sarge growled low, deep and sinister. He inched like a ninja to the front door. When someone knocked, the growl turned into a succession of sharp barks. The kind that happen just before a dog rips a limb from someone's socket.

Wes wanted to kill whoever was at the door. They were ruining one of the best moments of his year.

"This better be good, or I'm letting the dog eat you," he said as he swung the door open to find Cannon holding up a drunk Courtney.

"You said you didn't want her to drink and drive. I didn't know where to bring her. It was one of Sheriff Cooper's cells or your house."

"Hey, lover." Courtney stumbled into the house. "I'm home." She moved toward Wes but Sarge lunged in front of her with teeth bared. She stumbled sideways and leaned against the wall. "I hate that dog."

"Feeling looks mutual," Lydia said from behind Wes.

Now it was Wes's turn to growl. What the hell was he supposed to do with Courtney? He didn't have much choice but to let her stay. "Come on in."

Cannon looked between the two women. "Good luck." He disappeared before Wes could reply.

Ten years ago he would have killed to be the meat in the middle of two women.

Lydia went to the kitchen and returned with a glass of water and the bottle of painkillers. "Take two and drink all the water or you'll hate yourself tomorrow."

She walked back to the couch where she took up a seat in the corner and pressed Play for the movie to continue.

"Lydia and I are watching a movie, you're welcome to join us." Wes pointed to the chair next to the couch before he returned to his seat too far from Lydia. He hated the space between them.

Instead of sitting where he pointed, Courtney plopped down on the cushion next to him and laid her head on his shoulder.

Sarge's gravelly growl increased in pitch. Wes could have told him to stop, but the dog was showing the same discontent as he was with Courtney's presence.

"Move over, Courtney, I'm not your leaning post." When she didn't, he stood. "I'm going to bed."

Courtney popped up. "Me too then."

Wes shook his head. "Your bed is here." He pointed to the couch and tossed her the throw blanket that draped over the chair. "You'll have to wait until Lydia finishes her movie."

Courtney's lower lip popped out, but it wasn't cute like Lydia's pout.

"Why can't I sleep with you? We used to sleep together all the time." Her words slurred. She looked at Lydia and laughed. "We didn't get much sleep, but we shared a bed."

"Courtney, that's enough. It's the couch, or I'll call the sheriff and he'll be happy to give you a cot in his office."

"When did you get all grumpy?" She yanked the blanket and sank onto the end of the couch.

"That's my cue to leave." Lydia said. "Come on, Sarge." She stood and headed upstairs.

Wes turned back to Courtney. "When will you stop acting entitled?" He knew the answer before the question was complete. He enabled her to behave this way because he took care of her. For all intents and purposes he played the part of a husband without the benefits of the bed. "When you're sober, we need to talk."

"Wes, you don't want to talk." She stood up and pressed her body to his. "Let's do what we do best."

"That ship has sailed."

"It's back in port."

He glanced to the stairs. "Not interested."

"Is it the doctor? You want her?"

Wasn't it time he was honest with everyone, including himself?

"Yes. She's exactly who I want."

He left Courtney in the living room to fend for herself while he went upstairs, hoping to catch Lydia before she went to bed. But when he got to her door, it was closed.

CHAPTER FIFTEEN

Another restless night, but this one had nothing to do with the stress of not being where she wanted to be and everything to do with the man in the room next to hers. How could a single kiss change everything? She'd gone from a slobbering, weeping mess on the floor to a drunk kissed fool. Once again she'd picked the wrong guy. But at least Wes was honest about his intentions. He wanted forever, but maybe she could convince him that a moment was good enough.

Sarge lifted his head when she rolled out of bed but made no attempt to follow her. Lydia pressed her ear to the bathroom door hoping she didn't hear water running. Maybe hoping she did. There were worse things than seeing Wes naked. She couldn't think of anything better actually, but her poor luck held steady when silence greeted her.

She cracked it open to darkness and flipped the switch. Ahead, the door to Wes's room was closed. Part of her wanted to open it and see him still in bed. Was he the kind of man who slept in shorts or did he like the feel of bare skin and sheets? Did he sleep on his side, his stomach, his back?

Would he have a freight-train snore or did his breath escape in silence?

She palmed the knob and turned it only to find it locked from her side. Surely that wasn't to keep her out, since she could easily turn the button. No, it was to keep him out. Something about that pleased her. Wes had locked himself out of the bathroom, which meant he didn't trust himself to stay away. Maybe there was a chance for something short-lived after all.

Feeling lifted, she reached into the shower and turned on the jets. When the steam fogged the glass, she dropped her pajamas and stepped inside. It still smelled like citrus and Wes. The massaging jets hit every muscle on her body. They were like a lover's hands kneading her flesh.

She closed her eyes and imagined Wes's hands on her body, his fingers skimming across her skin. The heat of the shower with the heat of her fantasy had her throbbing with need.

She'd considered adjusting one of the pulsing jets to relieve the tension in her body when a gust of chilly air rushed over her skin.

"Change your mind?"

There was no reply, so she shut off the water. "I thought you weren't interested?"

"I'm not."

The high-pitched female voice surprised her. Courtney came into view.

"What the hell are you doing in here?" Lydia stepped out of the shower. The towel rack was just out of reach. She'd have to brush her body against Courtney to get to one.

"I had to pee, and this is the only working bathroom in the house." Courtney didn't move. She stood there and stared at Lydia like she was studying for an exam. "You're curvier than I would have imagined. Although you have little in the boob department." Her eyes focused on Lydia's chest. "I have a good plastic surgeon." Courtney pulled her top up to show a perfect pair of C cups. "I can give you his name."

"I'll pass. If you're finished, you can leave." Lydia moved from side to side trying to figure out how to get to a towel without touching Courtney.

"Did you think I was Wes? You know...he wants you."

"Not true."

"Hard for me to believe too. I may have been drunk last night, but he made it clear that he wanted you." Courtney leaned toward the mirror giving Lydia enough room to reach the hand towel. It wasn't enough to cover her whole body, but it would cover something.

"I'm sure you misinterpreted."

"Honey, there is one thing I'm rarely wrong about and that's men and their intentions. I've got eyes for guys. I'll tell you this. You won't regret one inch of him." She stepped to the door and opened it only to be stopped by Sarge. Teeth bared, he blocked her exit.

Courtney screamed and tried to slam the door, but Sarge pushed his way inside and cornered her by the towels.

If Lydia didn't know the dog to be sweet and docile, she would have feared for Courtney's life. By the way the woman screamed, it sounded like Sarge was ripping her to pieces when all he did was pin her in place with his presence.

Minutes later, the sound of boots stomped up the steps, and a shadow blocked the door between the bathroom and her room.

Standing in the center of the bathroom with nothing more than a hand towel to cover her was Lydia. She lifted the towel to cover her breasts, and when Wes's eyes went toward her lady bits she lowered the towel there. It was a game of either or in which she moved the towel to the spot his eyes focused on.

"Is someone going to get this dog off me?"

Wes gave Lydia a long appreciative look before he took Sarge by the collar and pulled him out of the room. He returned a moment later for Courtney. As he passed by the towel bar, he pulled a bath sheet free and handed it to Lydia.

"Not that I'm not enjoying the view. I am, but you look cold." His eyes rested on her pebbled nipples. "Are you up for some fun today?" He nudged Courtney out the door and closed it behind her. Once again Sarge showed his dislike with a growl.

Lydia wrapped the towel around her body. "I like fun."

When she was covered, Wes frowned. "Great. Get dressed. Put on a swimsuit under your clothes. I'm going to take you somewhere you'll love." He gave her a final once-over. "Breakfast is downstairs." He pulled the door closed after him.

Lydia leaned against the wall and let the towel drop. She'd air dried, anyway.

In the distance, she heard Wes and Courtney argue. He told her to get her stuff together and meet him in the kitchen.

Everyone loved to watch a train wreck. While Lydia didn't want to get in the middle of anything, she had a strong desire to see agitated Wes in action. So far he'd been kind and considerate, but everyone had their threshold, and it seemed Wes had hit his with Courtney.

While she brushed her teeth and hair and applied a little makeup, she wondered what she would have done if

Adam had shown up unannounced. Would she have given him a place to stay?

Laughter bubbled inside her. *He could have had the porch swing and a blanket.*

After rummaging in her bags for five minutes she found her bathing suit, which was little more than a string and three patches of fabric. Dressed in what could only be described as floss and Band-Aids, she looked in the mirror. Maybe that case of peanut-butter cups hadn't been the best way to ease heartache. She looked over her shoulder at her butt and confirmed that thought. With a tug on her bottoms she covered her tattoo and got dressed.

Downstairs, Wes leaned against the counter until he saw Lydia approach. By the time she entered the kitchen, he'd poured her a cup of coffee and plated up a banana nut muffin.

Courtney sat at the table with a just-ate-pickles look on her face. "You didn't get me a muffin."

"You're not my guest. Besides, you don't eat breakfast."

She didn't argue.

Lydia looked at Wes's ex-wife and couldn't see the attraction. She was pretty enough, but the minute Courtney opened her mouth, her beauty disappeared. Wes was gorgeous inside and out.

"Are you going to drive me to my car?" Courtney asked him.

He shook his head. "You're a big girl. You got yourself here, you'll get yourself there."

"I can take her." Lydia sipped her coffee and took a bite of her muffin. They were so good but what made them better was that Wes had left the house this morning and picked them up.

"Nope. We're leaving." He took Lydia's cup and transferred it to a to-go mug and wrapped her partially eaten muffin in a paper towel.

"You're leaving me here alone with the dog?"

Wes wrapped his arm around Lydia's shoulder and walked her toward the door. "You'll be okay," he said over his shoulder toward Courtney. "He ate and won't be hungry for a few hours. Besides, you're leaving."

He closed the door on her reply.

"We can't take Sarge with us?"

"Afraid for his safety?"

"Kind of."

"He can handle himself. Besides, this isn't a dog activity. It's a high-octane human endeavor." They rounded the truck.

"Dangerous?" She knew there was a glint of excitement in her eyes. There was something that happened to Wes when her emotions hit her eyes. He ate it up and smiled.

"Could be."

"Wait a second then." She raced to her car and pulled her first aid bag from the back seat. She went nowhere without it. "Better safe than sorry."

"I'll take care of you. You're safe with me."

For the first time in a long time she did feel safe. Not that she couldn't take care of herself. A part of her had had to grow up too fast. That was the part that still craved the love and care of another.

"Who will take care of you?"

Wes opened the door and helped her inside. "I thought maybe you could try it for the day."

Her heart thumped wildly. He was contradicting himself, which could only mean one thing. Wes had changed his mind about forever.

He climbed into the truck and backed out of the driveway. "Are you afraid of heights?"

"No."

"Can you swim?"

Lydia lifted her chin. "Butterfly champion at my school. Sage and I worked as lifeguards at the community pool when we were teenagers. I loved the high dive."

"You really are an adrenaline junkie."

Lydia settled in and watched the town fade from view. They turned onto the wooded county road that circled the big lake Aspen Cove was named after. She sat and finished her muffin and gazed at the still blue water. In the distance kayaks and small boats dotted the surface.

"Was it weird to have your ex-wife show up out of the blue?" She shifted her body so she leaned against the door and faced him. Positioned to see Wes, she took in his features all the way from his sandy blond hair to the T-shirt that hugged his chest on down to the shorts that left too much room for her imagination.

"It was more annoying than weird. She calls or shows up when she needs something."

"Hmm. That's not very nice."

He shrugged. "She has her moments, but the longer I know her the more I realize how rare the good moments are."

Lydia wondered if she should ask Wes about where this thing with them was headed. She liked her life nice and tidy. After her parents died all she thought about was life by design. If she could plan everything out and check off the boxes, then nothing could go wrong. Her premise was faulty. The last fight she and Adam had was over her concept of a tidy life. He'd told her, "Tidy was boring." What that really said was she was boring.

No risk, no reward. She heard her father's voice in her head.

"In the bathroom this morning, Courtney told me something." How could she ask him if he wanted her without sounding ridiculous?

"Disregard anything she said. She's finishing up college to be a lawyer, and the first thing they teach their students is how to lie. She had that mastered before she entered law school."

Oh Lord. She turned to the window and watched the pine trees rush past. *Back to square one with Wes.*

CHAPTER SIXTEEN

He pulled onto the soft shoulder of the highway. "We're here."

Lydia looked around her. "Where's here?"

"Prospect Falls." He climbed out of the truck and rushed to her side. When he opened the door, she slid from the seat. Her head bumped into his chest and settled there with her cheek pressed to his heart. He didn't give her much room to move. He wanted this moment to last a second longer because after he told her what they would do, she might not want to be near him again. Few women would jump off a cliff into a pool of ice-cold water.

"Okay, are we hiking?"

He stepped back and threaded his fingers through hers. "Something like that." He led her to the bed of the truck and opened the tailgate. Seconds later he lifted her up. "Hear me out. You said you were an adrenaline junkie. I'm giving you your fix." He slipped off her sandals and shoved them into a netted bag. Next went her shirt. He was struck mute when he saw her suit. "You're almost naked."

"Nothing you haven't already seen." She adjusted the

small cups of her top. The move made her firm breasts nearly fall out.

"Not true, that tiny towel you used today was like a retractable awning. I couldn't focus on anything."

"Right. Like I didn't see you staring at me." She reached out for the hem of his shirt and pulled it up and over his head. She tossed it on top of hers.

"Guilty as charged, but it went by too fast."

"Three's a crowd."

"Agreed." He unlocked the toolbox welded to the truck bed and pulled out sunscreen, a bag with sandwiches and bottles of water. "Now where's that EpiPen of yours? Bees have no address." There was no way he'd put her in a position where her life was in danger.

"Doc told me the same thing last week." She opened her purse and handed him her EpiPen.

"I told you he's a smart man." Wes wrapped her EpiPen inside a towel and shoved it into the net bag. "Wait here." He walked to the rocky edge that dropped off to a cool blue pool of water. He tossed the bag toward the clear shoreline on the right.

"What are you doing?"

"Prepping for our descent." When he got back to the truck, he shed his shoes and shorts. He pointed to her shorts. "You want to wear them or lose them?"

She shimmied out of the denim cut-offs. Her legs were long and toned. No doubt defined from years of walking hospital hallways. Her hips were rounded. Her waist was small. "So damn beautiful." He loved the way she soaked up his compliments. Her blush told him she wasn't used to flattery. That made it more fun.

"Are we hiking down barefoot?" She tried to jump off the truck. "I should bring my first aid kit."

"We're not hiking down." He lifted her to the ground and held her hand. "We're jumping."

She tensed for a second. "Are you crazy?" She rushed to the edge to watch the crash of the falls into the cove below. "That's a hundred feet."

Wes laughed. "Not so brave after all, are you?"

"I don't have a death wish. Have you jumped from here?" She inched to the edge again and looked over the side. Cold mountain water rushed from the mountainside into the lake. A light mist hung in the air and coated her skin.

"I do it all the time." It was his favorite thing to do once the snow melted. He generally waited until June when the water warmed up, but he didn't have until June. He had today. "You'll be okay."

She backed away from the edge. "You promise?"

"Yes. I promise." Her eyes danced with the sparkle of excitement, but behind that he saw trust. He imagined that after her experiences, she didn't give that easily. "Are you ready?"

"Will you go first?" She inched toward the edge.

"No way, lady. If I go first, you might chicken out, and I'd be by myself."

"I don't know where to jump."

He walked back to the truck and secured her bag in the lockbox. "We'll go together."

So she couldn't change her mind, he grabbed her hand and raced to the edge. She followed him without a hint of fear. They sailed through the air. What looked like one hundred feet was more like sixty. She screamed all the way down. It wasn't from fear but from excitement. Too bad he couldn't get her to apply her risk-taking attitude to the rest of her life.

They sliced through the frigid water together, sinking into the depths of the cove. They surfaced hand in hand with her spitting water. "Holy shit... holy shit..." she screamed as her body shook. "I didn't expect it to be so cold." She treaded water next to him, her lips turning blue. "Do you have any idea how dangerous it is to change your body temperature so quickly?"

He hadn't given it much thought. "Maybe we should go back to the truck."

She pushed away from him and swam to the edge. "No way. I'm ready to go again." She found her sandals off to the side, slid them on, and started the climb up the rocks to the top. Right behind her Wes got a good look at Lydia's perfect ass and the tattoo peeking above her swimsuit. He'd save that for later.

By their fourth jump, the water no longer seemed cold. "Come here." He swam under the falls and waited for her. She popped from below the surface.

Behind the curtain of rushing water were rocks smoothed by hundreds of years of erosion. He lifted her to a large boulder and told her to wait. He disappeared and returned with their lunch.

Wes climbed up next to her. He opened the plastic bag. "I've got a club sandwich or a tuna salad sandwich. Your choice."

She pointed to each sandwich in an eeny-meeny-miney-mo fashion before she said, "Let's share."

"Perfect plan." They sat together staring at the backside of the falls and ate.

"This might be the best day of my life," she said.

His heart pounded. "Better than all the days before today?"

Her smile reached her eyes. Light blue glitter sparkled from her irises.

She took long gulps of water. "It's been a long time since I've felt carefree. Longer since I've felt happy. There's only one thing that could make it better."

Wes looked around them. He had nothing else to offer. "What can I do to make it perfect?"

She moved closer. "Kiss me."

"Gladly." He pulled her into his lap and covered her mouth with his. It was a slow exploration. They weren't in a hurry to get anywhere. They had all day or at least until their bodies felt the cold again. But right now, he was hot. She made him hot.

Body to body, mouth to mouth, tongue to tongue, they shared a perfect kiss. Wes had to agree; it had been a long time since he'd felt this carefree. A long time since he felt this happy. And the kiss...it was perfect.

Like teenagers, they stayed behind the veil of water and made out until the cold reached their bones and the heat of their passion could no longer keep them warm.

"Shall we take this home?" she asked.

Wes nodded. "While I don't want to stop kissing you, I promised to keep you safe. Getting hypothermia is a real possibility."

She pressed her lips to his for a final kiss. "Ooh, such a big word for a country boy," she teased.

They stood, and he swatted her ass. "Let's go home and you can tell me about your tattoo."

"Fat chance," she said before she dove into the water and disappeared.

Wes gathered their garbage and followed her.

She beat him up the mountain but he liked the view. Her wet suit bottom clung to her skin, the light color telling him what she wouldn't. There was a smiley face tattooed to her right ass cheek. He knew that had to come with a story.

Once in the truck he turned to her. "Best date of my life."

"That was a date?" She covered her shivering body with the towel.

He turned up the heat. "I fed you and kissed you. I'd call that a date."

She peeked out from under the edge of the towel. "Best date ever."

"I owe you something else." He put the truck into drive and headed for Sam's Scoops. "You dropped your cone."

"It was a damn good cone too."

"A waste really."

"Kind of like the time you'd spend getting me ice cream when I'd rather go home for more kisses."

"That's why you're the doctor. Perfect diagnosis." He turned the truck around and headed for home. Although it was his house, having Lydia there felt right.

Hopefully Courtney had cleared out.

His hopes were dashed when he pulled into the driveway and found her sitting on the porch swing.

Lydia wrapped the towel around her body before she climbed out. There was no reason for her to be self-conscious in front of Courtney.

"Why are you still here?" Wes asked.

She pointed to her feet. "Your dog ate my shoes."

"He what?"

She rose from the swing. Her eyes took in their wet clothes. "Did he try to drown you?"

Lydia leaned into him and took his hand. He liked the show of ownership as if somehow she was claiming him. "No, we jumped off a cliff."

Courtney's mouth twisted. "On purpose?"

"Yes, and it was great," Lydia said.

"Umm, no thanks." She lifted a bare foot. "What are you going to do about my shoes? They were Pradas."

"Grab your shit, Courtney. I'll take you to your car, and I guess you'll drive barefoot because you're not staying here."

Lydia gripped the doorknob and turned it.

"Wait," Courtney cried. "What if he's waiting behind the door?"

Lydia swung it open to find Sarge sitting, with a half a shoe hanging from his mouth. "Did you miss me," she sang. The dog dropped the shoe and tackled her, covering her face with kisses.

"Why does he like her?"

"Sarge is a good judge of character. Now get your stuff," Wes said.

Courtney inched around the lovefest happening on the porch and snatched her purse and partial shoe.

"You owe me for this." She held up the half-eaten loafer.

"You want to tally things up? Don't forget our conversation this morning."

Before Lydia had made it downstairs, he'd broken the news to Courtney that he'd no longer be supporting her habits, good or bad. He wrote her a final check for her next semester of college and told her it was his last donation to the Courtney-loves-Courtney campaign.

Lydia hopped to her feet. "Will you be gone long?" The look she gave him made him wonder if she thought he wouldn't come back.

"Sweetheart, I'm not even stopping. Just rolling by slow enough so she can open the door and jump out."

Lydia laughed. "You should stop," she teased. "She doesn't have her Pradas."

Courtney huffed all the way to the car.

Wes bent down for a kiss before he left. He expected it to be quick. Not the case when their tongues touched and their hands wrapped around each other's bodies. They soaked in the warmth and passion each offered. It wasn't until the sound of his honking horn that they separated.

"Hold that thought," he said as he gave her another peck on the lips.

He climbed into the truck and slammed it into reverse.

"She's the one, isn't she?" Courtney dug inside her purse and pulled out a lipstick.

"I will not kiss and tell."

"I saw the kiss and I'll tell you. You never kissed me like that."

She was right. Wes pulled up to her car and stopped. "Good luck, Courtney."

"Luck? I thought you didn't believe in luck?"

He thought about Lydia. Wasn't it luck that brought her to his door? Her bad luck. His good.

"Take care of yourself."

She leaned over and kissed his cheek. "Thanks for being such a good man."

She hopped out of his truck and tiptoed across the asphalt to her BMW. Silently he said to himself, "Thanks for being out of my life."

He turned the truck around and raced back to Lydia.

CHAPTER SEVENTEEN

Lydia's skin tingled. It could have been from the cold or because her clothes were still damp. Most likely from the kiss though. When was the last time she'd experienced a toe-curling kiss like that?

Closing her eyes, she conjured up a memory of Adam and his kisses. They'd never done it for her. His kisses were too wet. Too sloppy. Wes combined the perfect amount of heat, wet and pressure to make her heart dance. Something told her things would get hot—fast.

Lake algae and sweat didn't sound all that appealing. It wasn't what she considered sexy by any means. With Sarge running after her, a Prada sole in his mouth, Lydia rushed to the shower. The temperature was reaching perfect when a light tap sounded on the door.

"You decent?" Wes asked.

She opened it still dressed in her bathing suit. "Yep. Still clothed."

"Darn." He snapped his fingers and leaned against the door. "I was hoping for less. Fewer clothes, that is. More of everything else."

Steam from the shower seeped over the glass and filled the room with an eerie foggy mist. It wrapped around them like wisps of smoke before it escaped out the door.

Her eyes traveled down his body. He wore nothing but swim trunks. His skin was tawny and tanned even though spring had just begun. Ripples of muscles begged for the touch of her fingers. Totally out of her league, Lydia wasn't sure how to proceed. She didn't have much dating experience. College had kept her busy. Medical school had been grueling. Residency had been...well, it had been all about Adam. What if Wes didn't like her? What if she was awful in bed? She had to be, right? Adam had never wanted sex.

Wes set his hands on her shoulders. "I see something happening behind those eyes of yours."

She rolled forward and put her forehead on the center of his chest. "I'm scared."

He moved one hand to her chin and lifted it. "I'll never hurt you. Tell me why you're afraid."

Could she be honest with him? Maybe the problem with Adam had been that they were never honest with each other. Wes deserved the truth. He'd taken her in and given her a place to live. He tempted her with his crooked smile, his carved-from-stone body, and his Pop-Tarts. Then again, how much honesty did a short-term fling deserve? "What if I'm bad in bed?"

His hand squeezed her shoulder. "Who told you that?"

"No one. I'm just thinking out loud. I mean, my last...he never wanted to...you know."

Wes moved forward, forcing her to step back. When they cleared the door, he closed it. "I want to, Lydia." He pressed his hips forward. His want poked the soft part of her stomach. "I want you."

How long had it been since she'd felt wanted? Probably

the last time she met Adam in the mop closet on the radiology floor. That was years ago.

Her fingers brushed over his chest, leaving a trail of bumps across his skin. "I want you too."

"Perfect." Wes lifted her to the granite countertop and stepped between her legs. "Just like you." He kissed her with such tenderness. All thoughts about inadequacy disappeared when his lips touched hers. When his tongue dipped inside her mouth for a taste. When his hands removed the clothes from her body.

He lowered her to the ground. She stood in front of him exposed and watched his face for any hint of disappointment. As his eyes traveled her body, so did the heat of knowing he wanted her. His gaze landed on the scar where she had her appendix removed.

He dropped his pants and showed her his. She hadn't noticed the faint white scar before, but who'd notice that when inches of pure male bobbed in front of her.

"Hurt like a bitch, right?" His fingers skimmed the faded line from her surgery.

Hers traced his. "The worst."

He looked behind her. "Care to share that shower?"

She'd forgotten about the water. "Oh my God, I forgot about the shower."

"Take a shower with me, and I'll make sure you forget about everything else."

Her knees turned to pudding, and she almost sank to the floor. If not for Wes wrapping his hand around her waist, she might have melted into the mosaic tiles.

They stepped inside the large shower together. The jets beat against their bodies.

"Did you get Courtney to her car okay?"

He squirted body wash in his palm and ran it over her

body. "No talk of Courtney. No mention of Adam. I won't share your body or mind with anyone else while we're naked. All I want to think about is you."

Slicked with soap, his hands roamed her body. One could argue that soap was sexy. Especially when slippery calloused hands moved across rock-hard nipples. When sudsy fingers pressed between her legs. Yep, soap was damn sexy.

Wes's touch was exploratory. He approached her body like an adventurer on an expedition. Curious hands, fingers, mouth, tongue worked their way over, under and inside her body. It was the inside she liked the most. When his finger pressed deep, she nearly came undone but then again he'd been touching her for ten minutes. Every cell in her body was on alert. Each nerve ending on fire. Wes was right, the only person she could think about was him.

When her hand closed around his length and a sigh of pure pleasure left his lips, her confidence soared. She stroked him and ate up the sounds she could pull from him with a kiss. His pleasure gave her power.

When the water went from steaming to tepid, Wes turned it off. He didn't give her much time to be disappointed. He wasn't finished with his exploration. He picked her up and took her to his bed wet.

"You can always say no, but I hope you'll say yes."

He moved her into the center of the big mattress and started at her toes. He licked the water from her body until he reached the apex of her thighs.

He stopped and gave her a look—one that asked if he could continue.

In answer to his silent question, Lydia's thighs fell open.

"Oh, God," she moaned when the flat of his tongue ran across her aroused flesh. Her fingers curled into his hair. All inhibitions left her body. She had no idea where this moment would lead. *Bullshit.* In minutes it would lead to him pressing into her body and her screaming his name. She wanted that. Needed it.

When he pulled the tight bundle of nerves into his mouth and sucked, she didn't care if this was only tonight. It was a minute of pure bliss. Just as her body trembled, he eased away and took the feeling with him.

"So close. I was so close." She wanted to cry. Her body shook from the pent-up desire. She was like a lava spewing volcano on the edge of eruption.

"I'll get you there, but I don't want to rush it." He climbed up her body and went to work on her breasts. He went from left to right until she squirmed beneath him.

"Stop torturing me."

"All right." He rolled off her body onto his back.

"What are you doing?"

"You said to stop torturing you. I stopped."

Lydia frowned. Not that he could see since they both were on their backs. She needed him on top of her. Inside her. If another hour of foreplay got her to the end goal, then she'd suffer through it. At that she laughed. "I'd like you to torture me more, please."

He chuckled, then reached into his nightstand drawer and pulled out a box of unopened condoms. He tore through the package and took out a strip. "This should do us for now." A minute later his hard length strained against the latex.

"For now?"

He climbed between her legs. "You think once will be enough?" He shook his head. "Not for me. I've tasted you."

He pressed forward and pulled back. He entered her little by little. Lydia wasn't used to big. Wes didn't rush her but allowed her body to adjust to him. He kissed her breasts, suckled her nipples, and moved to her mouth, where he made love to her with kisses. When he was fully seated inside her, he sighed.

"Never have I felt so damn good." His breath was labored and a sheen of sweat broke above his brow. "Damn, Lydia." He kissed her with such passion that her insides quivered. He wasn't even moving, and she reached climax.

"Oh God," she moaned as the undulating waves washed over her. When she looked at him, his jaw was tense.

"I'm holding on by a thread." He pulled back and pressed forward. Slowly he stroked every shudder from her body. When she finished pulsing around him, he picked up his pace. It didn't take long for him to get her to the edge again. It wasn't a surprise when he pulled out. Wes was into the long game. He didn't seem fixated on the end result.

"What are you doing?" she asked. Her body tightened and tensed.

"I'm learning you. Anything worth keeping is worth learning."

Her heart raced. He thought she was worth keeping. That brought warmth and fear. "You can't keep me." Her body hummed under his touch. God she wished he could keep her.

"You're mine for now, or do you want me to stop?" He cocked an eyebrow.

"That's not fair. It's like dangling a donut in front of a weak dieter."

"Take the donut, Lydia, you'll like it."

The heat of his breath almost took her there. "I'm so weak."

He chuckled. "I'll take that as a yes." He dove in and pulled her second climax with his tongue. Damn the man for having so much to offer. Most men excelled at something, but it would appear Wes was a master at most everything.

Her body lay limp and boneless when he entered her again. Languid soft strokes built up to powerful thrusts. From somewhere she found the energy to meet him thrust for thrust, and when that familiar rush of heat pooled in her belly, and the tingle of desire threaded through her veins, she soared over the edge with him.

He rolled to her side. Once he'd wrapped the spent condom inside a tissue, he folded his arms around her, pulled her tightly to his chest, and told her she was perfect. She felt like she was home for the first time in years.

She tried to convince herself that it was dopamine or endorphins. She was only experiencing the aftereffects of great sex, but she knew better. She liked Wes a whole hell of a lot more than she should.

This was her foray into something short-term, an encounter that was supposed to be meaningless and superficial. The problem was nothing about it was meaningless or superficial.

CHAPTER EIGHTEEN

How had this woman gotten under his skin in mere days? They said manufacturers of food had the perfect mix of sugar, fat, and salt down to an art to make a consumer crave more. Lydia's combination of vulnerability, strength, and compassion were the perfect combo to lure him in. Especially her compassion.

He'd watched her in action with Courtney. His ex had done nothing to garner Lydia's favor, but when she came in drunk, Lydia had gotten her water and painkillers. When they'd come home to find Courtney still at the house, she'd offered to drive her to her car.

Wes knew he'd fall hard and fast for Lydia but he didn't expect it to be this hard or this fast.

He drew circles around the smiley face tattooed to her ass while he watched her nap. It seemed fitting for the girl who handed out smiley stickers and ink marks to have one herself. There was a story to this tattoo he wanted to hear. One look at Lydia and she didn't come across as an emoji girl. He wanted to take a drive to Denver General and beat the pulp out of Adam for taking the smile out of her life.

If he couldn't persuade her to stay in Aspen Cove, then he'd settle for putting a smile back on her face. He'd seen her smile, and it was as bright as a nuclear explosion and almost as deadly because when she smiled, his heart seized.

"Higher," she moaned.

He flattened his hand and rubbed firm circles from her bottom to her shoulders. "You sore?" That didn't come out the way he meant it. He referred to jumping off the cliff into the water, but he imagined she was sore all over.

"Mmm." She rolled to her side, so they were face to face. "Yes, but it hurts so damn good."

His insides liquefied when her eyes lit up. Some people's eyes said more than their mouths. Lydia was one of those people blessed or cursed with expressive eyes.

He nuzzled her neck. "I can make you positively scream."

She ran her hand down his chest and gripped his hardening length. "You already did."

"Are you finished with me?" The words left a lump in his throat. He hoped she would not hop out of his bed and pretend what they shared wasn't beyond amazing. He'd had a lot of sex in his years, but sex with Lydia was the best. She responded to his touch. Her needy body gripped him like a damn vise. "I was hoping we could go for round two."

Lydia leaned back. Her laugh bubbled from deep inside. It vibrated through her chest and came out low and throaty. "You're only counting that as one? But I had three."

"The only thing I'm counting is how long it will take me to get back inside you."

She pushed him back and straddled his body. He was hard and ready. "It's my turn to give." The way she licked her lips made him twitch. Just seeing her on top of him caused him to ache everywhere. Never had he wanted a woman so badly. He reached for the condoms and tore one off.

She snagged it from his hand. "Not so fast. I'm in charge." She slid down his body and put those wet lips to work.

"Shit, Lydia." His hands went straight to fist the sheets. He didn't set the pace or the pressure with his hips. He lay back and enjoyed her superior skills. Like he'd done earlier, she teased him to the edge and eased him down repeatedly. "Can we stay here forever?"

She laughed around his length. The vibration nearly sent him over the edge. When she pulled away, he wasn't sure if he was disappointed or relieved. The torture of being kept on the edge was maddening but it was pure ecstasy.

Even rolling the condom on was sexy because she did it with her mouth. When she eased her body onto his length, he was lost. He fought the urge to turn them over take control. But this was her turn and he wouldn't take anything away from her.

Lydia found a rhythm that pushed her quickly to the edge, and thank God because he couldn't stop the unraveling that started at his toes and curled around his body until he burst inside her.

She fell forward with her head on his chest. This was perfect. So damn perfect.

HE WOKE and reached for her body but the sheets were cold. He rolled out of bed and rummaged through the pile of clothes on his floor for his jeans. Had she left his bed for hers? The short trip through the bathroom told him no. Her bed was empty, but the smell of something wonderful came from downstairs.

The savory garlic smell lured him to the kitchen, where Lydia stood in his yellow T-shirt and stirred the pot in front of her.

Her hips moved to a tune inside her head. He shouldered the wall and watched. "I've died and gone to heaven."

She swung around with a spoon in her hand. Red sauce dripped to the floor. "Oh shit." She looked at the spoon and the floor and back to him. "I'll get it."

Wes moved quickly to get to the towel before she could. "I got it." He kneeled and cleaned up the speck of red sauce. Once he'd tossed the towel into the corner, he rose slowly, running his hands from her ankles to her calves to her thighs until they skimmed her hips. "I missed you."

She lifted on tiptoes and kissed him softly. "We need to eat. If we're going to continue to exercise like that, I need food."

"I like that word *continue*."

"Me too, but food first. I hope you like spaghetti."

"Love it. How long have you been up?" The sun had set but the orange glow still lingered on the horizon. He guessed it was somewhere around seven.

"I couldn't sleep so as soon as you were out, I got up and came downstairs." She looked toward the table where her computer was opened and a pad of paper and a pencil sat nearby.

His stomach cramped with a fist-like punch. "Looking for a job again?" He tried to make his voice sound basic like her leaving was no big deal, but he knew it would be. She'd not only moved into his house but also his heart. "Any luck?"

Her deep sigh told the story. Inside he celebrated her defeat, which felt wrong on so many levels.

"There are a few things. A hospital in Tampa has shown interest, but they want letters of recommendation. I have some from other doctors, but no one who can truly attest to my skills."

She plated the precooked pasta and put a scoop of sauce on top.

"I can write you a letter and attest to certain skills." He took the plates from her hands and walked into the formal dining room. He hadn't eaten in here since he bought the place. One person sitting at a table this large only emphasized how alone he was.

"You think I have skills, huh?" She opened the oven and took out garlic bread.

"No doubt you have skills." He knew he didn't have sauce or pasta in the house, and definitely not garlic bread, so he'd add magician to her resume. "Did you go shopping?"

She sliced the crunchy French loaf into pieces. "Corner Store. This is the frozen stuff, but it's good. The sauce comes from a jar and the spaghetti a package. This meal is one step up from Sage's reheating skills. Let's eat."

Wes got a bottle of wine from the rack and poured them a glass. He sat at the end of the table with Lydia on his right. It was downright domestic. He looked at the four empty chairs and could see his children there. He shook the thought from his head. His heart was moving faster than his brain.

"Thanks for making dinner. You didn't have to do that."

She reached her hand to cover his. "I wanted to. You brought something out of me that's been buried for months, maybe years. My self-esteem had hit an all-time low."

Wes gripped his fork so tight his fingertips turned white.

"I know I said I didn't want to talk about Adam, but I think some things need to be said. I have questions if you're willing to answer them."

She pulled her hand back slowly. Was she distancing herself? When she reached for a piece of bread, he realized she was left handed and hungry.

"I have questions too. Lots, so ask away." She took a bite and moaned. "Oh my God, I'm starved. Even butter on cardboard tastes good."

Wes twisted ropes of spaghetti onto his fork. "No one makes jar spaghetti sauce better than you."

"You already got lucky, no need to flatter me." She sipped her wine.

"First question. Why did you stay with a man who didn't deserve you?"

Lydia swallowed and took another sip of wine. She seemed to need copious amounts of alcohol to loosen her lips so he topped off her glass.

"It's hard to say. There was the Adam I thought I knew and the Adam he really was. After my parents died" —she shook her head as if trying to get some vision to disappear—"things were bleak. I'd grown up to believe anything was possible, but in a second flat all my dreams died."

He moved his chair closer to hers and cupped her cheek. "I'm so sorry for your loss. I have parents I can't stand to be in the same room with."

"You never truly miss something until it's gone."

Wes sipped his wine and thought about her answer and knew it to be true. The biggest loss he suffered was when his grandfather passed away. He no longer had a man to shape and mold him into a decent human being. He only had his father who had decided long ago that Wes would never be enough. "Doesn't answer why you let Adam treat you badly."

"I'm almost embarrassed to tell you. In fact, I don't think I knew why until this second." She took a bigger drink of her wine. "I think I took what life gave me because at least I had something. Too afraid to challenge the universe, I accepted that I deserved less. Funny because I was raised to want more and in many things I demand it, but I didn't with him. Somewhere deep inside I knew he wasn't permanent and if I said anything, he'd leave me—which he did, anyway."

Wes pushed his almost empty plate away. "You deserve so much more."

"Advice coming from the guy who married a Bratz doll."

If she only knew he'd compared her to Barbie when he first met her. "I was a different person when I met her."

"Shallow? Superficial? Stupid?" She chomped into her last bite of garlic toast.

"Why do you think I was in charge of the park? Why do you think I'm in charge of building the Guild Center?"

She rolled her beautiful eyes. "Because you're the only construction guy in town?"

He leaned in. "You really think little of me, don't you?"

She grabbed her head. "I think about you all the time." She picked up her near-empty glass. "Damn wine. One glass in and my filter is gone."

He filled her glass up and put a splash in his. "I like you honest."

"What about you? Have you been honest with me?"

Wes considered her words. "I haven't been dishonest."

"Tell me why you married Courtney."

"My story is not too far off from yours, only my parents are alive but dead to me. As for Courtney, I was fighting my father's system, and she liked being my weapon. It's been a very expensive experience." He swirled the red wine in the glass. "I paid for her education."

"What? Why would you do that?"

The reason would make him seem like a saint but he wasn't. "I'd misled Courtney. She'd married an architect with dreams of living large and I changed the rules and showed her who I really was—a simple man with simple needs."

"You're an architect?" She twisted her head to the side.

"Was an architect. Award-winning, actually. You know that hospital in Colorado Springs where you wanted to work? I designed it. It was one of my first projects and honestly it was good but my problem was that nothing was ever good enough for my father. He loved that word *almost*. I've been trying to break myself from using it. It's an awful word."

"How the hell did you get so damn lucky? You're a Guild, an architect, a builder, hot as hell, have a big..." She caught herself looking at the zipper of his jeans and snapped her attention back to his face. "You kiss like a porn star, though I've never kissed a porn star, but you kiss how I think one would kiss. You know...someone with lots of kissing experience." She pushed the wineglass away. "Hell, if I drink any more I'll be telling you all my secrets and asking you to have my baby."

"Secrets I can do. The baby would be a neat trick."

"So you chose this life over having everything?"

He knew he had to pick his words carefully. "Lydia, I had a title, lots of money, a great flat in downtown Denver and a closet full of custom suits. I had a trophy wife, I drove a Porsche, and I hated myself. Be careful what you ask for—

you might get it and decide it wasn't everything you thought it would be."

"But I made promises. Promises I intend to keep."

It twisted his insides. No doubt those promises were made to people no longer present in her life. "Your parents would be proud of you. Hell, I'm proud of you, but the most important promise to keep is the one you make to yourself. What's the most important thing you want to accomplish in the world?"

Without hesitation she said, "I want to leave the world in a better place than I found it, and I can do that by being a good doctor."

"That's the promise you need to keep then. Nothing says you have to work at the Mayo Clinic or St. Jude. Good doctors are found everywhere, and you're one." He opened his palm and revealed his stitches. "You did this. You healed me."

"That was nothing." She squirmed in her seat.

"Nothing to you, but everything to me. That day you were a hellion wearing a halo."

"You did not just say that." She pushed from her seat and climbed into his lap. "Take it back."

He slapped his hand over her right ass cheek. "I'll take it back if you tell me why you have a smiley face tattooed on your ass."

CHAPTER NINETEEN

Lydia washed her hands and thought about last night. Who knew that an ass tattoo would be a conversation starter? Wes never let up. The only way to stop the endless questions was to take him to bed and tire him out.

"Last patient before lunch is here." Sage walked in and handed her Ray's folder.

"Again?" She didn't need to review it. The man had been here less than a week ago.

"Called this morning and said he was feeling tired."

"Again," she repeated.

The old man shuffled into the room. Rather than point to the exam table, Lydia pulled the corner chair forward. She grimaced when he fell into it and the legs creaked. Any minute she expected them to give way. Not because Ray was heavy but because the chair wasn't industrial strength. It was the type of chair a person could buy at an office supply store.

"What's up, Ray? Miss *60 Minutes* again?" She squatted in front of him. Her legs screamed in agony.

Between the cliff diving and the endless hours of Wes she was sore.

"Nope, got the whole show in." He wheezed, then leaned forward. "Got this here pain in my chest."

At the mention of chest pain, Lydia pulled out her stethoscope and listened. "Your heart rate is fast today, Ray. Are you exerting yourself too much?" She took his pulse and temperature and recorded the information.

"I walked in here, didn't I?"

"Yes, you did, and that's a good thing. I'd say more walking will do you good." She glanced back at a questionnaire he filled out at his annual exam. It noted that bacon and eggs were staple foods in his diet. He had a shot or two of whisky each night and smoked a half a pack of filterless cigarettes each day. "You need to cut out the bacon, booze, and cigarettes. I promise you'll feel better if you do."

His beard twitched. "Hell, if you take all the good things away, I might as well die. Next thing you know you'll be telling me to not have sex anymore."

"You have sex?"

Above his caveman beard, Ray blushed. "Betty from Buttercups in Silver Springs treats me real nice if I tip her well. Cheaper than a wife."

Lydia held up her hand. "I don't need details, but I'm glad you're getting..." What should she say? *Serviced? Laid?* "Sex is an important part of a healthy lifestyle, but it can put a strain on the heart if you're not in top shape."

He grabbed his rounded belly. "I'm in great shape. Ain't round a shape?"

She chuckled. "That it is, but seriously, Ray, you need to drop a few pounds. I'd love to see you walk around the new park a few days a week. Start slow and build yourself up."

His brows pinched together. "How about I schedule another visit to Buttercups each week?" He heaved himself to a standing position. "This getting healthy stuff will put me into the poor farm."

"Go for walks, Ray. Not getting healthier will put you into a grave. I'd like to send you to Silver Springs for some tests."

Ray walked toward the door. He waved her off with a fleshy palm. "I ain't no good at tests. Never was. Never will be."

Lydia stood in the center of the exam room and watched Ray shuffle out the door. "I don't know what to say." She made notes in his file to follow up on the medical tests. Explaining their importance today would only get her answers or stories she'd never get out of her head. As it was, she had a vision of Ray at Buttercups shoving dollars into the G-string of a grandma stripper.

She filed Ray's record and grabbed her purse. It was lunchtime, and she was starving. A familiar voice echoed down the hallway. Wes was here. Her heart raced at a giddy gallop. She wanted to run toward the store where she heard him talking to his aunt but played it cool. No matter how slow she wanted to walk, her feet skipped toward him.

When she rounded the sunscreen display, she saw him leaning against the counter talking to Agatha and Doc Parker, who manned the cash register.

As soon as Wes saw her, he smiled. God those lips were deadly. Whether it was a smile, a kiss, or something much sexier, the thought of his lips set her nerves alight.

"Hey, I thought you might be hungry?" He lifted a brow. "You got quite the workout yesterday."

Agatha huffed. "You're not making her sand floors or paint, are you?" She reached across the counter and grabbed his ear, pulling him closer. "She's already got a job." She gave his lobe an extra yank for emphasis.

Lydia thought it cute the way the red at his neck rose to his cheeks.

He shook his head. "No, Lydia and I—"

"Went cliff diving," she blurted. She wasn't sure what he'd divulge. The men in this town didn't seem shy about sharing their sexual encounters.

He nodded. "Yes, cliff diving takes a lot out of a person." That damn smile made her want to puddle at his feet. "Maisey's is open. They have tourist hours until the fall. Care to join me?"

Sage walked forward. "Room for one more?"

Lydia loved her sister but working together all day was enough bonding. "Don't you have a fiancé to bother?" She gave her a don't-crowd-me look and hoped her sister would bow out gracefully.

"You're right, he said he'd meet me at home for lunch." Sage tapped her head. "Next patient is Doc Parker. He's got your one o'clock slot but if you need more time, I can push him back." Sage gave Lydia a sly wink.

"One is perfect."

Doc Parker groaned. "I don't need you to look after me. I can diagnose myself."

Lydia walked ahead. "See you later, Doc. Don't be late." She looked over her shoulder to Wes. "You coming?"

From May through October the diner stayed busy but Maisey always reserved a table or two for the locals. She sat them in the corner booth. Today she delivered two iced teas without asking. Lydia had to admit it felt nice to have someone know her well enough to guess.

"How's your day going?" Wes asked.

"Oh you know, typical. One case of chicken pox that's

sure to spread through the entire town, a splinter the size of a log, common cold and obesity. How about yours?"

He sipped his tea and stared at her. Never had a man looked at her the way he did. She'd been too tired to put makeup on this morning. Barely got her hair pulled back into a ponytail but he made her feel beautiful.

"Typical, woke up to a hot-as-hell doctor. Went to work but got little accomplished because I keep thinking about that doctor."

"She's that hot, huh?"

"On fire."

Maisey delivered their blue-plate specials of fried chicken and mashed potatoes.

"What are you doing tonight?" Lydia held her breath, hoping he'd say he was doing her. Lord knew her body was aching and sore, but it also knew Wes was temporary and that meant she had to get her fill while she could.

"I thought I could fix you dinner and we could watch that movie you never got to finish."

"Not really in the mood for frozen pizza so how about I make dinner and we pick another movie? I've seen that one a million times so missing the end is no big deal."

"I've got skills beyond frozen pizza."

She licked her lips. "I know you do, but we can't sustain ourselves on those skills."

"Speak for yourself. I'm sure I could live devouring you."

Lydia looked around the diner. "Someone will hear you."

"So what. You want to keep me a secret? Well, then, you'll have to tattoo me to your ass."

"You're never going to let it go, are you?"

He shook his head. "Nope."

"Fine, I'll tell you while you're baking our frozen pizza, but it's not a great story, just an embarrassing one."

"No frozen pizza, and I can't wait for the story."

They finished their lunch and Lydia added pie. When they left, Wes walked her to the back entrance of the pharmacy so he could kiss her. She entered the clinic with a canyon-wide smile.

Doc was waiting for her in the examination room. Agatha sat on the chair in the corner.

Lydia listened to his lungs and prayed they were healing. They discussed his oxygen levels and agreed to cut it back and see how he responded.

Before they walked out, Agatha said, "My nephew is a good man."

Lydia wondered if her attraction to Wes was written on her face. "Seems to be. He's a nice guy." Best to keep it simple.

"He's a good catch."

Lydia walked Agatha to the door. "I'm not fishing."

"The best catch is when you throw out an empty hook and get a big one." She wrapped her arm through Doc's and led him back to the register.

The afternoon was filled with rashes, diarrhea, and one broken bone. She was about to send the patient to Silver Springs for an X-ray when Sage opened a closet that wasn't actually a closet but an X-ray machine. Maybe the clinic wasn't archaic after all.

At the close of business, Lydia drove home. It was odd to call a temporary place home, but it felt like it to her.

When she opened the door, she braced herself for Sarge, who raced down the hallway and skidded to a halt at her feet.

"Hey, boy. Did you miss me?" She ruffled her hand

across his fur and followed the smell of barbecue to the kitchen. The room was vacant so she followed her nose to the back door and found Wes standing in front of a barbecue by the pergola.

Lydia opened the door and Sarge raced out.

Wes sidestepped the fur ball. "Welcome home." He pointed his beer toward a small cooler at his feet. "You want one?"

"Let me change, and I'll be right there." She raced inside and put on jeans and a T-shirt. It was May, which meant when the sun went down so did the temperature. It wasn't unusual for the nights to hit near freezing. When she returned to the backyard, he was sitting in the pergola. He'd set up a table with candles and flowers.

"Is this a date or are you trying to get lucky?"

"Yes."

"Yes?"

"It's a date and I hope I get lucky. Now tell me about that tattoo."

CHAPTER TWENTY

Wes handed Lydia an open beer and rose to check on the steaks. He'd run to Copper Creek to check on permits and stopped by the store to pick up a few necessities like beer, coffee and condoms. Somehow two T-bones had ended up in his cart along with corn on the cob and potatoes.

He loved that Lydia had a big appetite. There'd be no going out and throwing half of her food away. Hell, she'd probably clean her plate and eat half of his before she moved on to dessert.

"How do you like your steak?"

"Make sure it doesn't moo when I cut into it. I like it medium to medium well."

"You got it." He flipped the meat and came back to the table.

Lydia played with the flowers he put in the center. "Where did you learn how to barbecue?"

If she thought she was getting out of telling him her story by deflecting, she was wrong. "The Bishops barbecue on the beach all the time. Hell, even in a snowstorm. Katie told me how to prep the corn by buttering it, adding salt and pepper and a few basil leaves, then wrapping it in foil." He got up and took the seat next to hers. "Where'd you get your tattoo?"

She cracked her neck the way a boxer would before a fight. Wes looked at her hands to make sure they weren't fisted. She was peeling the label off her beer.

"I'm a sure thing whether or not you get it off in one piece. Now tell me."

"You're relentless."

"Some would call that an attribute."

"Or annoying. But fine, you want a story. I'll tell you a story. My first year of residency I worked with a nurse, and I kid you not, her name was Sally Slaughter." She laughed. "Yep, you heard me right, Nurse Slaughter. She was somewhere between fifty and dead. One foot planted in the ER while the other looked for an ass to kick. She was one mean, crotchety old lady."

"So you liked her."

"More than I like you right now." She got the label off and handed it to him like it was a gift certificate she intended to redeem. "I decided early on that it was my mission to change her from foe to a friend."

"Continue." He rose and checked the steaks and turned the corn. The potatoes he'd microwaved earlier and kept warm at the back of the grill.

"She hated me. I don't know if it was because I was sleeping with the boss or what, but she rode my ass the entire first year." Lydia drank her beer and sat forward. A sparkle of mischief danced across her eyes. "I called her the SS because she ran the ER like a Nazi, and those were her initials. She was the first to call me Satan because she said my presence made her job feel like hell."

"Okay so you had a pissing fight with her. And?"

"I'm getting there. Don't rush me."

He plated the steaks, which might have been a mistake because if Lydia was eating she wasn't talking.

The sun began to set so Wes plugged in the lights that twinkled around the pergola. To see the amazement and appreciation in Lydia's eyes was worth the hour spent hanging them.

"These weren't here yesterday. Did you hang them for our date?"

"I did."

"Why are you treating me so well?"

He walked to her and pressed a kiss to her forehead. "Because someone needs to show you how you should be treated. Set the bar high, Lydia, and settle for nothing less." He took his seat and watched her soak in his words.

"I am. That's why I want to work in a big hospital. What does working here say about me?"

He wanted to beat his head against the beam at his back. That was not the message he tried to convey. Sure, he wanted her to be happy with her work. If that meant long hours and little appreciation, he'd support her decision, but he recognized himself in her. The light in her eyes died when the subject of where she'd work came up. It returned when she talked about the work. The problem was Lydia didn't know herself well enough to see it was the work that mattered, not the location.

"Working here says you're a good sister and a good friend. The lives you save here are no less important than the lives you'd save at a big hospital. But that's not what I'm getting at. While you're here, I want you to know what it feels like to matter to a man. You matter to me."

She swallowed hard twice and looked the other way. "Back to my story."

It was obvious Lydia didn't deal with emotions well. Wes imagined losing her parents at sixteen was a factor. There was so much he wanted to know about her, but he didn't want to push. "Yes, finish your story."

"SS never smiled. So I made a bet with a fellow intern named Taya. If I got Sally to smile by the end of our first year, then Taya had to get a tattoo of my choosing."

"I see where this is going. What would you have put on Taya's ass?"

"A skull and crossbones so she would never forget Sally Slaughter, but I lost and so Taya insisted I put the smile I could never get from Sally on my right cheek."

"What shocks me is you did it."

"I'm a woman of my word." She took a bite of her steak and hummed. "You want to hear the worst part of the story?"

"Worse than having a permanent emoji on your ass?"

"Turns out Nurse Slaughter was in on the ruse. She made sure to never crack a smile while I was around. She said every time I looked in the mirror and saw that tattoo I could imagine her laughing at my stubborn ass. After I found out, I dropped my pants in front of her and told her to kiss my happy ass. From that point forward, I had a passion for all things smiley. And guess what?"

"I can't imagine."

"Nurse Slaughter never stopped smiling at me from that point forward. It was more of a laugh than anything else. By the end of my third year, she'd become a friend. Since I'd set out with that goal in mind, I came out a winner and got a free tattoo."

"Personally, I love that tattoo. It makes me feel lucky to know you're smiling when you arrive and you're smiling when you leave."

"What about you? What's the silliest thing you ever did?"

It didn't take him long to answer. "Marry Courtney."

"I said silly, not stupid."

While Lydia emptied her plate, he thought about silliness. It wasn't allowed in his family. "I guess I don't do silly. In my family it was never allowed. I was a Covington. Covingtons were taken seriously." He lowered his voice to mimic his father's.

"Nothing silly? You never even TP'd a house?"

He shook his head. "I'm ashamed to admit it, but no."

"Eat up, mister, we've got mischief to make."

After the dishes were done, Lydia gathered every roll of toilet paper in the house. She donned black clothes and convinced Wes to do the same. He couldn't believe she'd talked him into vandalizing property.

"How about Sheriff Cooper's house?"

"Are you crazy? If we get caught, we'll end up in a cell."

She lifted onto her tiptoes and kissed him. "I've never had sex in a jail cell. If we get caught, I'll rock your world." She picked up the bag of toilet paper and walked toward the front door.

Wes adjusted the bulge in his jeans. He was one sick bastard to get turned on by the thought of sex in a jail cell, but it wasn't the cell that excited him. It was Lydia.

They drove around town until last of the orange sunset dipped behind the peak and the cloak of night fell around them.

"Are you sure this is his house," she whispered. "He's got flower pots and shit. Doesn't come across as the guy who likes to garden."

"Coop has a real green thumb. You should see the

vegetables he grows in his back yard. Maisey gets a lot of her produce from him for the diner."

"Hmm. I would have never thought he'd be a gardener."

Wes pulled to the end of Jasmine Lane and killed the engine. "I say we sit here and make out like teenagers."

Lydia made a *pfft* sound and exited the truck. She pulled the hoodie over her blond hair and grabbed the bag of toilet paper from the back.

Wes joined her.

"Are you scared?" she teased. She placed her hand over his pounding heart. There was no doubt it beat faster and harder than normal. Part from the fear of getting caught, the other part from knowing Lydia was near. And although it was almost pitch black outside, he knew if he could see her eyes they'd be dancing with delight. While he fed his adrenaline junkie, she taught him to let go.

"What do we do?"

"Not get caught." She hunched over and slipped through the night like a ninja. Being six-foot-two, hunching made Wes normal height. "When we get there, we'll each take a roll and toss it over the branches of his big oak tree." She rubbed her hands together like a mad scientist. "We've only got ten rolls so we have to make them count. Go for the lower branches so we have more visual impact."

"There's an art to this?"

She stopped at the vacant house next door. "Yes, if we didn't like the sheriff, we'd aim for the highest branches. It would be a bigger hassle for him to clean up. If we hated him, we would have waited for the forecast of rain or egged his house. You're just a beginner so we have to start small and work our way up."

"There are levels?"

She stifled a laugh. "I have so much to teach you."

They quietly tossed rolls over the lower branches until the sheriff's big oak resembled an over-tinseled tree. As soon as they finished, the front porch light turned on and Wes was certain they'd been caught. While he stood like a deer caught in the headlights. Lydia ran down the block.

When he reached her, she jumped into his arms and wrapped her legs around his waist. "Ever made love in public?" she asked. Her lips crashed against his. While he held her bottom, she grabbed the edge of his T-shirt and pulled it over his head. They stumbled to the truck and climbed into the back to make a bed from their discarded clothes.

Lydia was trouble. Not only had she stolen his good sense but also his heart. How could he deny her when she asked for so little? In that moment, all she wanted was him.

He made love to her under a million stars without a care in the world. And when they were satisfied and spent, he pulled her body over his and stared toward the cloudless sky.

"What's next?" he asked.

She turned into him and placed her head on his chest. "That wasn't enough?"

"More than enough. I should have..." Adrenaline mixed with arousal had made his release explosive. He hadn't considered anything but pleasing her. He'd acted impulsively. "Used a condom. I'm sorry."

"Not your fault. We got caught up in the moment and it was beautiful." She hugged him. "Don't worry, I'm on the pill. There's no need to panic."

Getting Lydia pregnant was the farthest thing from his mind when he filled her body. Even now, the idea didn't scare him in the least. In fact, he'd already seen their children in his dreams. Little girls with wavy blond hair. A son with her big, blue eyes.

"I wasn't worried, but that's good to know."

"It's just...most men would freak out. I want you to feel safe. I've been tested and I protect myself."

"Not very well. What if I had a disease?"

"You don't. I checked your record, and you were tested a few months ago. Since you always have a condom handy, I figure you are Mr. Safety with everyone."

"Are you even allowed to look at my file?"

She pinched his side. "Yes, I'm your doctor."

A cool breeze wisped over their naked bodies. Wes inched out from under Lydia and reached for their clothes. "Aren't there rules against doctor-patient relationships?" If she said yes, he'd gladly transfer to a doctor in Copper Creek.

She pulled her shirt over her head. "You make me want to break all the rules."

Right there at the end of Jasmine Lane, Wes experienced many firsts. First time he'd TP'd a house. First time he'd had sex on a public street. First time he'd not used a condom in his life. It was the moment when everything changed. When pressing himself inside Lydia turned from sex to making love.

CHAPTER TWENTY-ONE

Her eyes flew open when his lips pressed against hers.

"I'm heading to work. Have a good day." Wes looked damn right sinful sitting on the edge of the bed in a black T-shirt, with his scruffy beard and wet hair. She'd asked him to not shave because she loved the feel of his whiskers on her neck.

In a sleepy voice, she asked, "Are you working at the Guild Center?"

He brushed the hair from her face. "We will frame today. This is where it gets exciting. It's so much fun to watch it all come together."

She cupped his cheek. He was the sweetest man she'd ever met. "I'm so excited for you. I can see you're exactly where you want to be."

He licked his lower lip in that sexy way that made her body tingle. Something about it made her want to strip him naked and have her way.

"Where I want to be is buried inside your body, but where I need to be is at work. You want to have dinner together?"

She let her hand drop to the bed. "I'll cook since you cooked last night."

"Sounds great. See you tonight, sweetheart." He brushed his lips to hers before he left. As soon as Wes disappeared, Sarge took up his space. He pressed his furry body close to hers and went to sleep.

She listened to the door close downstairs. All this time she'd been hoping for the universe to cut her a break. It seemed as if it did when Wes came into her life but if karma ever smiled on her again and sent her a decent job, she'd miss him terribly. Not only was he gifted between the sheets but he had the biggest heart she'd ever seen. What man paid for his ex-wife's college? What man volunteered to design the fire station and the park? That man was Wes, and he did it because the people around him mattered.

An hour later, Lydia got up, showered, then went downstairs. She followed her normal routine of answering emails, applying for jobs, and paying bills. Her student loans were killing her. She had the money to pay them back if she used the profits from the sale of her house, but if she drained her account, she wouldn't have the money for a new place once she got to wherever her forever was.

Working at Doc's clinic didn't pay enough to cover her expenses and her loan payments. It was a choice between live comfortably now or comfortably later. She hovered over the payment button. One click and her loan would be gone. One click and she'd be living paycheck to paycheck. Was it better to borrow from Peter to pay Paul? *Screw Peter.* She pressed the button and watched the money move from her checking to her loan. In seconds she was the proud owner of a fully-paid-for medical degree. Something about that felt so grown-up.

She needed to tell someone, so she headed to the

bakery. It was Tuesday and that meant cranberry orange muffins.

Katie was putting a fresh batch in when she arrived. "Good to see you, Lydia. How are things?"

Lydia generally held her emotions close to her chest but things were good and she couldn't hide the smile. "Considering I'm broke and homeless, I'm good."

"Speaking of homeless, Abby came back early and plans to harvest her bees this week. I'll have to see to some repairs to drywall and stuff, but the apartment should be ready in another week or so."

"Oh...okay." Gone was her smile. She knew she'd have to leave Wes eventually, but she wasn't ready to give him up yet.

"How's Wes been treating you?" Katie handed her a cup of black coffee and the daily muffin across the counter. "You two seem to get along."

Her smile was back. The mention of Wes warmed her insides. "He's been awesome. He's such a nice guy."

Katie stared at her. "You really like him, don't you?"

Her cheeks heated. "He's a nice guy."

"Right, a nice guy who kisses like a porn star." She picked up her cup of coffee and rounded the counter to join Lydia at the front table.

"My sister has such a big mouth." Lydia pulled her phone from her purse and texted.

I'm at the bakery and you're in big trouble.

Two minutes later Sage texted back.

On my way.

"So, shall we wait for your sister to talk about the sex or do you want to give me the dirty details right now?"

"I won't kiss and tell."

"Yes, you will. Girls need to know. I won't rush on

getting the apartment back together if your current situation is satisfactory."

Lydia laughed. "More than satisfactory."

"I need the details."

Sage pulled up in front of the bakery. When she entered, she walked behind the counter and got what she wanted. That was the beauty of being best friends with the owner. Then again, Lydia knew she could do the same. Somehow, she belonged or at least they treated her like she did.

"What am I in trouble for now?" Sage took the seat across from Lydia. She knew it was to gain distance from the sure-to-come pinch.

"Porn star?"

Sage frowned at Katie. "There are no secrets in a small town."

"That's not something a guy wants to hear from a neighbor?" Lydia asked.

Katie shrugged. "I guess it would depend on the neighbor. I imagine he'd wear it like a badge of honor." She turned to her sister. "We were just going to discuss whether his porn star talents ended at a kiss."

"We were not." Lydia buried her face in her hands.

"Oh, please. I've told everyone Bowie is bait on my hook. Samantha says Dalton strums her like a fine-tuned instrument. Sage says Cannon is best at sex on the beach."

"Your man is in construction. Give us a pun that's telling," Katie begged.

Lydia pursed her lips. In a quiet voice—almost a whisper, she said, "Wes can really hammer it home."

An outsider might have thought they'd won the lottery with the way they laughed and giggled and high-fived one another.

"So does that mean you're considering staying?" Sage looked hopeful.

Lydia hated to ruin the fun. She knew the importance of family. Sage was all she had, but Sage couldn't say the same. She'd built a life and a new family. The family she chose besides the one she had.

"No, I'm not staying."

Sage slumped forward. "You're so frustrating. Let me tell you, the grass isn't greener on the other side."

"How would you know?"

"Because I lived on the other side in your basement. I worked and slept and worked and slept. It was an endless circle of nothing. How sad is it that the best part of my day was passing you on the way to work when you'd bring me coffee?"

Lydia thought back to those nights when she'd walk in the door while Sage walked out. She'd seen more of her sister in the past week than she had in those few years. She'd moved through life on autopilot for so long she had no idea how to steer.

"Your priorities are skewed. They have been since Mom and Dad died."

Lydia's eyes grew wide. "Not true. My priorities were you and Grandma. I had to step up and take the reins until Grandma Dotty could. I had to grow up overnight so you could have a childhood."

Sage grumbled. "Not true. While Grandma and I grieved, you buried your hurt and never addressed it. Time passed but somewhere deep inside you're still sixteen. Trying to get that A on your report card so someone can be proud. Geez, Lydia, no one gives a shit where you work but you. If working eighteen hours a day and coming home to nothing is what you want, then I'll support it, but I've seen you smile more in the last week than the last decade."

"So..." Katie broke in in an attempt to avoid a sister showdown. "Did you hear someone TP'd the sheriff's house?"

Lydia looked at Katie. The memory of last night eased her agitation. When Sage said she'd smiled more in the last week than the last decade she recognized the truth in that statement.

"Let's not fight. It's been an interesting week for me. Don't forget that in the last month, my dreams were dashed, and I was thrust into Small Town USA. It's like being dunked in ice water. While startling at first, I am getting used to it." She turned to Katie. "Did you say TP?"

The next hour they came up with a suspect list. Katie thought it was the Dawson's oldest son. Sage said it was probably his deputy Mark getting back at him for something. All the while Lydia drank her coffee and ate her muffin knowing she and Wes were responsible.

Wes...what the hell was she going to do about her growing feelings for a man she couldn't keep? It wasn't as if staying in Aspen Cove was a possibility. Soon Doc would be well enough to run his two-day-a-week clinic, and Lydia wouldn't be needed. A startling thought occurred to her. She wanted to be wanted. That's why being turned down by a dozen hospitals hurt so much. She needed to be needed.

She rose from her chair and gave both girls a hug. "I've got to go. Sarge is alone at the house and he probably needs to be let out."

Both women looked at her with lifted brows. "That sounds domestic. Are you making dinner too?" Sage asked.

She yanked one of her sister's curls. "Let it alone, smartass. I'm staying at his house for free. The least I can do is let his dog out and fix a meal or two."

Katie laughed. "The least for sure. Tell the porn king we said hello."

"Now look who's never grown up." She walked to the door and turned. "I adulted today and paid off my student loans. That means I'm broke." She stopped to consider how she felt. "But, I'm happy."

The bell above the door rang as she walked into the sun. Main Street was bustling with a dozen or so patrons. People moved between the Corner Store, Maisey's Diner, and the Dry Goods Store where locals sold their handcrafted goods. There were only two vacant properties on the street. One used to be a beauty parlor, the other a tailor. She closed her eyes and pictured one as a Starbuck's. While Katie's Keurig was fine, nothing beat a triple espresso.

When she got home, she played with Sarge and then read a book before she started dinner. It was the second best day of her week. The first being Sunday when everything between Wes and her became more.

Tonight she made salmon with steamed broccoli. She didn't decorate the dining room with tiny twinkling lights but she set the table and brought the flowers in from the pergola.

When Wes walked in all sweaty and dirty, she'd never imagined she could feel so content. He kissed her and asked if he had time to shower before they ate.

She turned the oven off and joined him.

CHAPTER TWENTY-TWO

Wes sat on one of the folding chairs in the hallway of the clinic waiting for his appointment. There were eight seats and all of them full. If Lydia thought for a second her services weren't needed, all she had to do was peek out the door and see the crowd.

Sage came out looking frazzled and pointed to him. "You're next."

He rose from the first chair and entered the examination room.

"I don't think you need supervision. I'm running across the street for a coffee. I'll bring one for you both."

Sage closed the door behind her.

"You okay, sweetheart?" Lydia looked exhausted. Could be because they'd made love all night.

"Five cases of chicken pox this morning. I told you the whole town would have it. You've had them, right?"

"When I was six."

She opened a drawer and pulled out a white bag containing scissors. "Have a seat, Mr. Covington. Let's get these stitches out."

He sat on the exam table and closed his hand over hers. "Take a minute and breathe."

She rested her head on his chest. "I feel like I'm back at the ER and there's an epidemic happening. There's nothing I can do. It's a virus and it has to work its way through the system, but I'm worried about Katie with her heart and Doc with his suppressed immune system. It's going through Louise's house like an out-of-control fire and she's pregnant."

"Breathe, baby. They'll be okay." He lifted her chin and kissed her. The tension left her body.

"How do you do that with a kiss? You're like Xanax. Can I keep you?"

That was the question of the day, not whether she could but if she would. "I'm all yours."

She took a deep breath and let it out. In true Lydia fashion, she scrubbed her hands until he was certain she'd have no skin left, donned gloves and opened the sealed bag. She carefully cut and tweezed the sutures from his palm. When they were gone, she brought his hand to her lips and kissed his palm.

"I'm so glad you lost the battle with that window."

"Me too."

They both knew that a chance accident had set them on a path to meet each other.

"Seems like between the cut and the bees, the universe wanted us to meet."

She snuggled into him and kissed his neck. "I'd call that luck."

He laughed. "I won't argue with you."

She stepped back and cleaned up. "Because I'm right?"

He shook his head. "No. Because you pinch hard."

She grabbed the pebble of his nipple and twisted. He let out a yelp that no doubt was heard in the hallway.

He held her hand to stop the torture. "Hey, everyone in the hallway will think I'm a wimp."

She tossed the used instruments into a holding bin. "No, they won't. Rumor has it you kiss like a porn star."

After a minute of shock, he laughed. "Who's telling my secrets?"

"My sister."

"But I've never kissed her," he teased.

"You better not unless you want more stitches."

She took his hand and yanked him off the exam table.

He pulled her into his arms. "The only woman I want to kiss is you." He kissed her like he had all day even though he didn't. When he pulled away, her soft satisfied smile told him everything was all right in her world. "I have to go to Copper Creek. How about I bring home a pizza?"

She wrapped her arms around him. "I could fall in love with you if I let myself."

His heart nearly exploded. She had put *love* and *you* in the same sentence when referencing him. The order of words was wrong and there were several extras that were not needed, but the sentiment was there. He was making his way into Lydia's heart.

"Let yourself and see where it gets you. You might be surprised." They walked to the door.

She put her hand on the knob but he stopped her from turning it. "I have this friend who told me he had his heart set on going to Paris. It was his dream to spend the week photographing the Eiffel Tower, but the French Transportation Department went on strike and he had to cancel the trip."

She tilted her head in confusion. "So where did he go?"

"Nowhere, he stayed and took pictures in Arizona where he lived. He spent the week visiting famous landmarks like the Grand Canyon and looked at life through a different lens. The interesting thing is he sold those pictures to *National Geographic* for a small fortune. He'd caught images of wildlife and landscape that no one had seen before. My point is he would have never seen what was possible if he'd gone to Paris." Wes gave her another kiss and walked out the door.

The rest of his day wasn't as pleasant as suture removal and kisses. He had to deal with Craig Caswell, who held up the final permits for the new fire department because he wanted to feel in charge. Each day the crew was on standby the fund lost thousands of dollars.

"I don't understand what the holdup is," Wes started. "I've filed all the plans. I've got everything but your signature."

The asshole smiled. "Yep, and nothing happens without my signature."

The intercom buzzed. "Mr. Caswell?" a woman asked in a shaky voice.

"What?" The plaques on his wall shook.

"Umm...your wife is here and insists on seeing you."

"Send her in." A choking-on-bone cough came from Craig. "My stupid wife has an emergency."

The hair stood on the back of Wes's neck when Craig referred to his wife as stupid. He hated bullies and if evil had a mascot, Craig Caswell would be the poster child.

The door opened behind him and in walked a beautiful brunette, who scanned the room like she was walking into a den of lions.

She turned to Wes, "I'm sorry to interrupt your meeting. I'll only be a moment." She slapped a flash drive on the desk in front of him. "I thought you'd like to see this. Your father was fascinated. He said to come by the house tonight."

Craig gripped his wife's wrist so hard her hand turned purple. Wes stood ready to intervene when she flipped Craig's wrist and took control. She bent it back until he growled. If this was their foreplay, Wes didn't want to witness the act.

"I should be going. If you just sign the permit, we can get started. Aspen Cove needs a fire station."

Mrs. Caswell let go of his hand and gave Craig a forceful jab to the ribs. It wasn't like the pinch from Lydia that eventually led to a kiss and then bed. This woman had something to prove or something to say. "Sign the form, Craig. Isn't it time you stopped holding people hostage?" She pressed the pen into his hand and walked away.

Craig Caswell did the unthinkable. He signed the permit, then shoved it across the desk.

Wes didn't wait for him to change his mind. He swiped the page into his hand and bolted from the office before Craig could reconsider. Wes made a promise to himself that if he ever ran into Mrs. Caswell again, he'd give her a hug.

An hour later he was home with a pizza and a bottle of champagne—an odd combination for a celebration, but having the permits signed for the firehouse deserved something special. He found Lydia in front of her computer no doubt looking at employment sites.

In his right hand he held the pizza box, in the left was a bottle of high-end bubbly.

"Pizza and champagne." She closed her computer and pushed it aside. While Wes uncorked the bottle, Lydia served the pizza. They took their plates to the pergola and watched the sun set while he told her about his day.

"That's awesome. Maybe after the fire station, the town will get a real medical clinic."

That comment interested Wes. "We have a clinic. What's it missing?"

"You want a list?"

He leaned forward. "Yes, I do. What would make the clinic perfect for you?"

She took a bite of the crust. While she chewed, Wes could see the gears in her brain working. Her head moved from side to side as if she were walking the space for real.

"First, I'd separate the pharmacy from the clinic. You can't really call a place that sells over-the-counter drugs a pharmacy and not laugh. I'd create a real waiting room with comfy chairs. There would definitely be more than one exam room. Having only one room is inefficient. There should be more than a closet dedicated to radiology." She sipped her champagne.

"There's a radiology closet?"

She nodded. "Shocking to me too. I thought we had to send all potential broken bones to Copper Creek but Doc has an X-ray machine. A decent one at that." She picked a piece of pepperoni off her pizza.

"So what is our clinic lacking?"

Her jaw tensed then relaxed. Her eyes squinted then softened.

"Nothing really. It has everything it needs, but it's put together wrong. I mean there's only a corner for infection control. He's got a small autoclave for sterilizing instruments. That should really be in a contained space."

"So what you're saying is Doc has everything a competent doctor needs. The problem for you is it's not put together in a way that makes sense."

She gathered the empty plates and set them in the

center of the table. "It's not about what I like, it's about efficiency."

"Having everything in one room doesn't make it efficient?"

"No, it makes it crowded. Who wants to trip over a patient to toss contaminated instruments into a holding bin?"

"What you're requesting is a remodel. It wouldn't take building a new clinic to get what you want."

"It doesn't matter anyway because what I'd want is irrelevant. It's Doc Parker's clinic." She emptied her glass and stood. "Let's plan who we'll vandalize next." She skipped all the way to the back door with Sarge following behind hoping for a chance at leftovers.

When Wes entered the house, Lydia was at the kitchen table with a pencil and paper. At the top was the word *hostage*. He knew he was in trouble. Lydia was upping her prankster games.

"I'm not kidnapping anyone."

She bumped his shoulder and leaned into him. "No silly, we'll hold items hostage for ransom." She jotted down her sister's name first and next to it she wrote *carved bear*.

"That's got to be illegal."

"Yes, it's stealing, but this is stealing for the greater good. For example, if we steal the welcome bear from the bed and breakfast and hold it hostage until let's say Sage and Cannon sponsor the softball team, then lots of people win. People will figure out that losing something means someone else wins."

"So you want to do something bad to get something good?"

"Wouldn't that be fun?"

"You're diabolical. What else do people do to prank others?"

"It's limitless. You can toothpick or fork a yard. That's where you stick thousands in the grass. I've filled cars full of foam peanuts."

"You're mean." He pushed the list away and pulled her into his lap.

"I've got a streak, but you can also do pranks because you love someone. My college roommate opened our dorm room door once and found a curtain of Sour Patch Kids because they were her guilty pleasure. My favorite, and so romantic, is the story of the guy who covered his girlfriend's car in Post-it Notes filled with all the reasons he loved her. It took five thousand notes to cover her Civic. That's love."

"That's crazy?"

"That's commitment," she sighed.

"Or requires commitment...to a loony bin. Five thousand Post-its?"

CHAPTER TWENTY-THREE

Lydia raced up the stairs with another hostage. She put the pink flamingos next to the garden gnome who shared space with the welcome bear. The spare room was full of items borrowed in exchange for silly demands like mowing an elderly neighbor's yard. The adult and children's softball teams had uniforms and Doc had sponsored mammograms at a clinic in Silver Springs.

Over the past three weeks. Lydia and Wes had donned their dark clothes and snuck around in the black of the night. They exchanged a letter typed on pink stationary that stated demands for the return of the hostage.

The talk around town was Bea Bennett's ghost had come back to Aspen Cove. Lydia loved how they could perpetuate one woman's gift into a symbol of caring for a small community whose motto was "Aspen Cove takes care of its own."

When Bea died, she'd gifted her estate on pink stationary. Not everyone got a gift. Most got a request to help a neighbor out. A few got life-changing presents. It was how Sage ended up in Aspen Cove. She'd cared for Bea during her final days and Bea gifted her the bed and breakfast telling her Aspen Cove needed someone like her. Katie got the bakery because of her connection to Bea's daughter Brandy.

No one cared anymore if their silly yard art was missing. It became a sense of pride to come out and find a pink envelope taped to their door. It meant the resident had something to offer the community.

"Our house is being taken over." Wes walked in and wrapped his arms around her waist.

She liked the way he referred to his home as theirs. They'd adapted to a routine of sorts. On the days she worked he cooked. The other weekdays she made dinner. Weekends were spent eating out, stealing from their neighbors, and making love.

Wes took her rappelling on Mount Meeker. Her heart nearly beat out of her chest when she backed off the cliff. He seemed to get her as a person, and as a woman.

Each day she opened her email praying that a job offer would be there, yet hoping that one wouldn't.

On one hand she wanted to be wanted, to be sought as a valuable team member. With Wes she felt she was needed. Like somehow, if she disappeared, his life would be less. She was torn between want and need.

"Speaking of home," Lydia said. "Katie called and told me my apartment was ready."

Wes put his hands on her shoulders and turned her around. His lips stretched into a thin line before he spoke.

"Do you want to move back to the apartment above the bakery?"

No! "I don't want to be a burden to you or overstay my welcome." She looked down at the dog, who leaned into her side as if not touching her would kill him. "If I stay much longer, Sarge will no longer be yours."

Wes laced his fingers through hers and led her to their bedroom. Little by little her stuff had moved from the room next door to his. Their clothes intermingled in the closet. Their socks shared a drawer.

He lay on the bed and pulled her to his side to face him. "Let's clear a few things up. You're not a burden. I didn't know what to expect that first day because, well...we didn't get off to a great start, but honestly, it has been great. Spending every night curled up next to your body is amazing." He tapped her nose with his finger. "If you want to move back to the apartment I'll support that. Don't get that confused with liking it."

She tilted her head. "I'd rather stay here."

"I want you here. You belong with me."

Lydia's heart skipped a beat. He didn't say she belonged to him, but it was close and she liked it. It wasn't like she was going anywhere else. Her options were still limited, but what she had was pretty damn good.

"Thank you." She pressed her lips to his for a soft kiss.

Sarge walked into the room and crawled into his dog bed. While he could sleep with Lydia in her bed, there wasn't enough room for the three of them in Wes's, so he was banished to a dog bed in the corner. He showed his discontentment with a loud huff.

"You're wrong if you think he belongs to me. He became yours the day you let him in your bed."

Lydia snuggled into Wes's side. "I became yours the day you let me into yours."

"Watch out, Lydia, you're sounding like you may stay."

"Watch out, Wes, I might."

WHEN LYDIA ARRIVED at the clinic, she expected to see Ray in the first chair. He'd been her Monday morning patient since she started but he wasn't there.

Sage's face looked grim, which could only mean two things. She hadn't had enough coffee or something was wrong. Since she had her "Nurses do it all night" coffee mug in hand, Lydia knew something serious had occurred.

They entered the exam room alone and shut the door.

"What's up?"

Sage leaned against the counter nearly knocking the liquid sterilizer container to the ground. "It's Ray."

"I'm not doing a house call." Last Sunday night Lydia answered the door to find Ray there stating he had an emergency. She rushed for her first aid kit only to find his emergency was 60 *Minutes* was on and his cable was out. He sat there for the whole hour watching Wes's television eating Jiffy Pop and drinking root beer.

"You won't need to. He died last night."

Lydia stumbled back. "How?" Be a doctor long enough and lots of patients will die, but Lydia had only been in Aspen Cove for a month and one of her regulars was already gone.

The door opened and Doc Parker slipped in. "Has Sage told you about Ray?"

Lydia was speechless. This was her fault. He'd shown all the signs of heart failure—exhaustion, shortness of breath and chest pain.

Doc moved to the corner chair and took a seat. "It's not your fault."

Lydia hopped onto the exam table for support. "But I knew he was struggling."

"Did you tell him to lose weight?"

"Yes."

"Did you tell him to exercise?"

"Well, I told him to walk around the park. I was worried about anything more strenuous."

"Did you tell him to get an EKG in Copper Creek?"

"Yes, I even made the appointments and called to remind him. I offered to drive him."

Doc stood and came over to Lydia. He turned to Sage. "Hand me a stethoscope."

Sage grabbed one for the Doc. He rubbed the metal end against his palm.

She leaned back. "What are you doing?"

"Proving something." He placed the ear tips in her ears and set the drum against her chest. She heard the *thump, thump, thump* of her heart. "Hear that?"

She nodded and pulled the ear tips from her ears.

"That's the sound of compassion. I see it in everything you do. You have a big heart and it's bound to hurt when you lose a patient." He tapped against his chest and coughed. "I've told him a hundred times to lose weight, to give up bacon, whiskey and cigarettes. You know what he said?"

"If you take all the good things away, I might as well die," Sage and Lydia said together.

"And he did."

"Was he alone?" Lydia wasn't certain of Ray's home life, but she imagined he lived alone.

Doc chuckled, then masked his smile. "He was at Buttercups. Poor Betty sent him on his way with a smile. I'd say if you have to go...he went well."

Sage gasped. "That poor woman." She covered her mouth.

Lydia wasn't certain if her sister was laughing or appalled.

Doc shook his head. "Word has it she's unhappy she didn't get her tip."

"Oh Lord." Lydia hopped off the table. "I'm sorry you've lost a patient, Doc Parker. It hurts my heart because Ray was a good guy. Seems to me there are worse sins than bacon, booze, and babes."

Doc walked to the door. "The babes will do it to you every time." He turned to look at the sisters. "It was hard for me to let the clinic go but you girls run a tight ship. Hell, we're so busy I'm going to open another day to keep up with demand. Hope you're not going anywhere, Lydia. At my best I can do two days a week. No way I'd be able to work full time."

Lydia rolled her eyes. "What's wrong with this town? Three days doesn't make a full-time job."

"Tell me that when you get to your seventies. Stick around, you're needed here."

"It's not like anyone else is knocking down my door to hire me."

"Idiots," Doc said as he walked away.

Lydia turned to her sister. "Who's first?" While she would have liked to take time to mourn the loss of Ray, a peek into the waiting hallway showed the chairs full. All women.

By the end of the day, Lydia had seen more vaginas than most men. Turns out the women of Aspen Cove had put off their annual female exams because Doc was like a father and no one wanted to show their goodies to their dad. Aspen Cove needed her. Not because she was a good doctor but because she was a woman doctor.

At closing she packed up her things and walked to the front, where Agatha held a stack of cheesy casseroles.

"Please tell me one of these is tamale pie." Lydia didn't know who brought the tamale pie but it was her favorite.

"It's on top." She followed Lydia to the door. "How are you and Wes?"

"We're good. He's a good man." It was funny for Lydia to consider her and Wes a thing. It didn't start out that way, but she couldn't imagine them not together. He'd become a necessity in her life.

"Yes, he is. I'd say he's more Guild than Covington. The Guilds always put people first while the Covingtons...well let's just say Wes's father isn't a Guild."

"So glad he took after his Aunt Agatha."

"Are you sure you're not a Guild?" the older woman said.

"Nope, I'm a Nichols through and through, but I imagine you and I aren't that different."

"I'm smarter by about forty years." She patted her shoulder as she pushed her out the door. "We're also humble." Agatha's laughter halted as soon as the door closed.

Lydia walked to her car and thought about her parents. She was raised to value people more than money, possessions or power. A lump lodged in her throat. Somewhere along the way she'd forgotten who she was. When had she decided she needed a title more than she needed love? When did the value of working in a big hospital outweigh the value of working in a community? Aspen Cove needed her, and if she was honest with herself, she needed Aspen Cove.

CHAPTER TWENTY-FOUR

Despite only a few hours of sleep, Lydia looked stunning in her little black dress and heels.

"You ready?" They were off to attend Ray's funeral.

After an hour of deliberation last night, they gave Ray credit for the hostage taking not because they were placing false blame but because the act was the talk of the town. People loved the idea of doing something bad for good. Lydia wanted people talking about Ray for his good nature as opposed to the way he died.

As a man, Wes argued that dying with a pair of breasts in his face wouldn't be a bad way to go.

Lydia won out, which meant they snuck all the hostages to the cemetery. In Aspen Cove, everyone turned out for weddings, funerals and park openings.

He helped her into the truck and gave her a kiss. "You okay?"

"Yes, I feel bad I couldn't do more to save him."

Wes shut the door and rounded the truck. When he climbed inside, he turned to Lydia. "When I told you that Doc's daughter blamed him for not saving her mother, you said you can't save everyone. Are you exempt from that equation?"

She buckled up and stared out the window. "No, but knowing doesn't make the loss easier. He was a nice enough man."

When they arrived at the cemetery, at least two dozen residents hugging their lost treasures greeted them. Hearing several people mention it was nice to know Ray had such a big heart confirmed that their decision to give him star status was a good one.

As with any get together in the small town, when the funeral was over, they headed to the bar, where the Bishops donated beer and the town folk brought the food.

People who knew Ray best said a few words, and the sheriff ended the celebration with a reminder to not drink and drive. Before he gave up the mic, he said he was glad someone returned the lost items. He stared at Wes and Lydia, who hadn't thought to steal something of their own in order to blend in with the other victims.

It never occurred to the others to think Ray had an accomplice. Funny how several dozen items could show up at the cemetery and no one questioned where they came from. Then again, Sheriff Cooper was trained to catch criminals.

"Anyone know who TP'd my house?" His eyes never left Lydia and Wes. When he hopped off the tiny stage used for karaoke, he headed straight to them.

Wes shoved his hands inside his pockets, hoping it would make it more difficult for the sheriff to cuff him. Maybe he could convince him to wait until after the celebration of Ray's life.

He nodded. "Wes." He looked to Lydia. "Dr. Nichols. It's good to see you both."

Lydia smiled, but one look at her dilated pupils and he knew she was nervous.

The sheriff leaned in and spoke softly. "While I don't condone theft, I can see the value of a little prank, but why couldn't you steal something from me rather than TP my house?" He set his hand on the butt of his pistol and Lydia's eyes grew wide. "That shit took hours to clean up."

Lydia looked at Wes. "We have no idea what you're talking about."

Sheriff nodded slowly. "Right." He set his hand on Wes's shoulder. "I hear you're handy and I've got security cameras I'd like installed. Shouldn't take you longer than an hour." He looked between the two. "I figure you owe me that much."

Wes laughed. "I'll be over tomorrow."

Sheriff Cooper stepped back. "You're a good man, Covington." He nodded toward Lydia. "This one's going to be trouble."

"She already is, Sheriff." Wes slid his arm around Lydia's shoulder and pulled her against him. "The thing is... I like trouble."

"Never a dull moment." The sheriff moved to the buffet table.

"So, I'm trouble?" She leaned into him and they fit together like puzzle pieces.

In his heart he knew she was the one. "Trouble with a capital T, my love." He hadn't meant to call her that. Hadn't really considered what he felt but his love was undeniable. It hit him as fast and as hard as the chicken pox virus had hit the town, but this wasn't something that would go away with rest and time.

"Your love?"

They made their way to the food table, where Wes

handed her a plate. "Can't deny it anymore. I feel about you the way I feel about chicken wings." He tossed a few hot wings on his plate and moved down the row.

"How do you feel about chicken wings?"

He reached back and grabbed another one. "After one taste I always want more."

Lydia opened her mouth to respond when her phone rang. She rummaged through her bag and pulled it out. She turned the screen to show him it was Memorial Hospital calling.

The silver specks in her eyes sparkled.

"I've got to take this." She pressed Answer and moved outside.

Wes watched her from the window. He saw a range of emotions crossing her face, from confusion to elation. When she turned and saw him looking at her, he knew right then, she'd been granted her greatest wish. She'd been offered her dream job.

She hung up and paced the sidewalk in front of the window.

Wes tossed his plate of food into the trash can and moved her way. This was one of those moments he wanted to be selfish and tell her she couldn't go. If she left, she'd take his heart with her.

He was stupid to fall in love with her. She'd been clear from the start what her goals were. How many times had she told him she wanted more? All the anger he'd felt over the years at being almost enough burned inside him. Just once, he wanted someone to choose him for who he was and what he offered.

"Let's go." He didn't mean for his voice to be so stern and unyielding. It wasn't like him to take his frustrations out on others, but he'd risked so much with Lydia and by the look on her face he knew he'd lost it all.

"Go where?" She twisted the strap of her purse around her hand.

"Home so you can pack."

"You don't even know what that was about." She swung her purse in a circle, almost taking him out twice.

"Give me that before you hurt someone. Namely me." He swiped her purse from her grip. "I know they offered you a job. I know you better than you think. Your eyes light up like sparklers when you're happy. Watching you was like watching the Fourth of July. Are you telling me I'm wrong?"

She lowered her head. "No, you're right. The person they hired didn't work out."

"Let's go then." He walked to the truck and tossed her purse inside. "I'm sure they want you there right away."

"Why are you in such a hurry to get rid of me?"

"Because I know I can't keep you."

Wes jumped in his truck and started the engine. The deep throaty sound of the diesel growled louder than he could so he gunned it and let the cloud of black smoke speak for his mood.

"You don't get to decide for me, but it would have been nice for you to fight for me," she yelled loud enough for him to hear.

By the faces pressed to the bar window, he wasn't the only one listening. He rolled it down and yelled, "Are you coming or not?"

She looked between him and the crowd gathering in the window. "No, I'm walking. I need to think." She took off down the street in her four-inch heels.

"You're so stubborn." She was already halfway down

the block and didn't hear him. All he wanted to do was get her into the car and kiss her until she forgot about everything but him. Instead, he drove home, knowing she'd need to soak her aching feet when she arrived.

When he got there, the first thing he did was dial her number to apologize, but he had her purse and her phone. He'd have to wait until she got home to make amends.

He had no reason to be angry with her. She'd never lied to him. He'd taken a chance she'd change her mind, but when he saw that smile on her face, he knew the job was what she wanted, or at least what she thought she wanted.

While he waited for her, he poured her a glass of wine and ran her a bath. No doubt even a few blocks in those heels would be torture. Ten minutes passed, and then fifteen. When it got to thirty he worried. Back in the truck, he drove the route he knew she'd take. A block from the house, he found her lying on the ground, lips blue and unresponsive. A large red welt took up the right side of her cheek. She'd been stung.

Wes panicked. On the sidewalk by her side he shook her. Her breath was wheezy and shallow. Thankfully she was breathing.

Shit, shit, shit, shit. How long did she say she had until death? He raced to the truck to get her purse. Dumping it on the seat he found her EpiPen. As soon as the syringe was in his hands he raced back to her.

Paste white, she looked dead. Maybe he was too late. "Don't you die on me. We still have to argue about you leaving me."

He glanced over the directions, pulled the shot out of the cylinder. The dizziness overwhelmed him. Stars danced in front of his eyes. He removed the cap and realized the needle was hidden. With a firm grip he held the pen, exposed her thigh muscle and injected her for a count of ten just like it said on the label.

When he was done, he scooped her up, put her in the truck and raced to the clinic. People were milling around outside the bar. When Wes double-parked in front of the clinic, he yelled for help. Seconds later Sage and Doc rushed toward him.

Lydia was awake but dazed. Her lips were literally bee-sting swollen. Her cheek looked like she'd been on the losing end of a prizefight. None of that mattered because her chest moved up and down and her hands gripped his shirt like she'd never let him go.

As soon as the pharmacy door was unlocked, Wes raced her to the examination room and laid her on the table.

Sage had oxygen on her sister quickly. She took her pulse while Doc listened to her heart.

Lydia tried to sit up, but her sister pushed her down. "You need to stay put."

Her tiny pale hand lifted the mask from her face. "I'm okay." She looked at Wes with such sadness in her eyes. "Thank you."

"You don't have to thank me. I'm so sorry. I shouldn't have left you. I was hurt and afraid, but never more afraid than finding you lifeless and thinking I was too late."

Doc tapped Sage on the arm and motioned for her to follow him out.

"You saved me." She pulled at the table mechanism to get the back to lift.

"Let me do that." Wes adjusted the exam table so she was sitting. "You should go to the hospital."

She looked down at the clip Sage had put on her finger. It flashed red with the number eighty-five. "No, I'll be okay. Doc will make me wait until I get over ninety-two to go home, but I will, I bounce back pretty well. I'll just be tired."

She patted the space beside her and Wes took a seat and pulled her against his chest.

"You scared the hell out of me. This is my fault. I had your purse. You could have died."

She buried her face against his chest. "Not your fault. Sometimes..." She shook her head. "I don't respond with maturity. My sister reminds me I got stuck at sixteen when my parents died. I'm impetuous and childish."

"I love you anyway."

"You love me?"

"As much as I love chicken wings."

CHAPTER TWENTY-FIVE

Wes tucked Lydia into their bed. He even let Sarge sleep beside her. These were the men in her life. Both loving and protective.

"It's meatloaf Thursday, I'll pick up dinner at the diner later." He went to leave and Lydia stopped him with a touch.

"Please don't leave me." She pulled him down next to her. "I don't want to be alone." It was silly because Lydia had spent most of her life alone. She was used to being alone but she didn't like it. Even when she lived with Adam and Sage, she'd been alone. They all moved through their lives like ships in the night. Passing off Starbucks and hugs when they met in between.

He cupped her cheek and kissed her. "Doc said you should rest."

"I am resting, and I'll rest better if you're here."

He looked torn. "I'm here for you."

"The call..."

"We don't need to talk about that right now." He pulled her close to him so her face was against his chest.

"We do." She pulled back and looked into his eyes. "They offered me the job I'd applied for, but I don't know if I want to take it. They didn't choose me first. Makes me feel like I'm on the B team."

He rolled to his back, and she rested her cheek against his chest. Beneath his breath, she heard his heart race.

"They were idiots. They chose poorly the first time around and now they're being smart."

She wrapped a leg over his leg and an arm over his stomach. Nothing like a brush with death to make her feel uncertain about everything—almost everything except him. That was the one thing she was positive about. She loved him. She had no intention of leaving him, no matter how much she'd wanted the job originally. Did that make her fickle? She didn't care. What she cared about was how comfortable it was to lie in his arms.

"I don't want to go. I lo—"

"Don't say it, Lydia, because if you do, I'll never let you go." He nudged her off his chest and rolled to his side so they were face to face.

"I don't want you to let me go." She tried to snuggle into him but he held her in place.

"You have to go. I can't keep you here."

His words hit her like a boulder to the chest. "What do you mean?"

He took several deep breaths before he spoke. "If you don't go, you'll never know if it was the right choice. In the back of your mind, you'll wonder what if?" He ran his hand down her side, resting his palm on her hip. "I refuse to be another person's *almost good enough* when I want to be someone's *everything*."

"But you are."

He shook his head. "Lydia, from the moment you

stepped foot in Aspen Cove all you talked about was leaving. I set my sights on making you want to stay. That was selfish of me."

"You succeeded. I want to stay."

"Until you get a taste of what you asked for, you'll always wonder. I never want to be a regret. You need to go. You didn't tell them no already, did you?"

That question broke her heart because she didn't tell them no. She told them she'd call them back, which meant in the back of her mind she was still considering the offer.

"No." She swallowed the answer like bitter medicine. "I wanted a day to think about what I wanted to do."

In his eyes she didn't see anger. She didn't see hurt. She saw nothing but understanding. "That's why you need to go."

"Why can't you be selfish and tell me to stay?" Tears came easy to her in her exhausted state. They slipped silently down her cheek.

He brushed them away. "Because what I want may not be what you need. I walked away from my family business. It was the most selfish thing I've ever done. My father didn't beg me to stay. He told me if I left I could never return."

"That's awful." Her parents pushed her to be the best. It was part of her driving force but had she failed at something, they would have never turned their backs. In that second, she had an epiphany. She'd been lying to herself all these years. Telling herself success would honor her parents. Even if she'd failed, they would have been proud that she'd tried.

"I chose. I walked away from a successful career because I needed to know if I could succeed on my own. I did. You need to go to Colorado Springs and see if your dreams are there."

He was right, but he was wrong too. "You're part of my dream. I want it all. I want you and the hospital and everything."

His eyes turned soft and sad. "I belong here."

Lydia cupped his face. "You told me you love me. Ask me to stay and I will."

Wes pressed his lips together. "It's because I love you that I want you to go."

Lydia knew she lost the fight when he rolled off the bed and left. She wanted to call after him and tell him because she loved him she'd stay, but he'd already stopped her from saying the words. He was right. All it would take was their next argument for her to wonder if she'd made the right choice. He knew her better than she knew herself.

She slept the rest of the day. Woke to join Wes for diner takeout only to fall asleep again. When she got up the next morning, Wes was gone. He'd made her coffee and left a tented note beside it.

Call Memorial. They won't wait, but I will.

Love,

Wes

What did he mean he'd wait? Surely he wouldn't wait forever, but she loved him even more because he put her needs first. She also hated him that he didn't demand she stay. She picked up her phone and made the first call to her sister.

"You feeling okay?" Sage asked.

"No. I'm not." She felt sick to her stomach. Was it excitement or anxiety that twisted her gut? Maybe it was that Wes loved her enough to let go or maybe it was he wouldn't fight for her. She was conflicted.

"Shall I get Doc?"

She sipped her now-cold coffee. How she slept past ten didn't compute. She'd gotten lazy living in Aspen Cove.

"No, it's not that. I didn't have a chance to tell you that Memorial Hospital called and offered me the position. It was what Wes and I were arguing about when I stomped off and got myself stung."

There was a length of silence followed by, "Oh. So when are you going?" Sage's tight voice asked. "You are going, right?"

"I have to." She had to know for sure.

"Perfect. Just when we're opening the clinic to three days."

"I'm sorry. You knew this was temporary."

In the background, she heard the familiar sound of Sage's microwave beeping, which meant something awful had finished cooking. Most likely lasagna.

"I thought you'd stay. I mean you and Wes..."

"He told me to go." Just saying the words made her heart hurt. She closed her eyes and imagined a day without him. Everything inside her ached, from her brain to her stomach, with the biggest pain felt in her chest.

"What? Are all men assholes?" Sage mumbled something about commitment and love.

"Wes isn't an asshole. He's probably the most unselfish man I've ever known."

"Ouch, shit." The sound of Sage blowing on something filtered through the line. "Sorry, burned myself."

"You okay?"

"Yes, just pissed that he didn't fight for you."

The same thing had crossed Lydia's mind a time or two, but telling her to go was fighting for her. "He wants me to be happy, and he knows I'll always wonder if I don't take the chance. He's putting me first. Not sure I've ever had a man do that."

Sage sighed. "I get it. I get why you have to go, but I don't have to like it. I don't have to like him for supporting you because something tells me if he asked you to stay, you would. You may not be willing to admit it yet, but I see you look at him. You love him."

"I do and I love him even more because he's willing to let me go."

"What if you get there and hate it?" Hope hung on each word. Lydia knew Sage didn't wish her bad, only bad enough to get her to come back to Aspen Cove.

Lydia opened the back door to see if Sarge was on the porch. He was nowhere in sight. This would be her new norm. No dog. No boyfriend. No coffee. No notes. Her only hope was that the job was perfect. Exactly why she'd spent eleven years training.

"What if I get there and love it?"

"When will you leave?"

When Lydia spoke to the head of HR yesterday, they seemed pretty desperate. "Probably over the weekend."

"Shit, shit, shit."

"Burn yourself again?"

"No. Now I'm just pissed that you're leaving."

Lydia walked around the house while they spoke. She loved the old place. The way the floors creaked and the trees outside rustled. The old dining-room table that spoke of a family to Wes. After he told her his father disowned him for leaving, she could see why refurbishing his ancestral home was so important. It symbolized everything he'd lost.

"I'm only a few hours away. It's not like I'm moving to another country." Lydia went back to the kitchen and put her cup in the dishwasher. If she planned to leave tomorrow, she needed to pack.

"I know you, you'll bury yourself in work and never have a minute to visit."

No doubt Lydia would bury herself in work but it would be so she wouldn't have time to miss Sage and Katie and Samantha and Doc and mostly Wes.

When he came home from work that night, her car was packed. They spent an hour at Bishop's Brewhouse, where karaoke was a town ritual. Lydia told everyone how wonderful they'd made her life in Aspen Cove.

That night, Wes made love to her. There was no place where he ended and she began. Connected by their bodies and heart and minds, they were one.

The next morning he kissed her goodbye. By the time she reached the edge of town she couldn't see through her tears. Each mile she drove made her mind muddy and her heart heavy. She tried to remember why it was so important for her to leave when all she wanted to do was stay.

Wes's voice kept her foot on the gas pedal and her car pointed south. "If you don't go, you'll never know if it was the right choice. In the back of your mind, you'll wonder what if."

It was a no-win situation because now that she'd driven out of Aspen Cove, her mind kept asking, *What if I'd stayed?*

CHAPTER TWENTY-SIX

How sad was it that the best part of his day was waiting for a call from Lydia? She'd literally hit the ground running. With twelve to fourteen-hour shifts, she didn't have the time to house hunt. He hated her living in a rent-by-the-week hotel room, but this was a journey she needed to travel alone.

Sitting on the couch with a glass of wine, he stared at his phone, silently begging for it to ring. Even Sarge had looked forward to her calls. Wes would turn on the speaker so the dog could hear her voice. He'd get excited and then lie by the front door for hours waiting for her to come.

Wes hadn't washed her pillowcase since she left two weeks ago. It still had the faint smell of her peach shampoo. He buried his face in it each night before he went to sleep.

When her face popped up on the screen, he didn't waste a second to answer it though he toned his excitement down. The last thing he wanted was to appear pathetic.

"Hey, how's it going?"

She laughed. "I don't know if I'm coming or going. All I do is work and sleep."

"Living the dream." He hated that her life had turned into less and wondered if she saw that for herself.

"It's a nightmare. Big car accident today. Three dead, and two who won't ever be the same."

"That's awful. The worst thing going on here is Bailey Brown and poison ivy. I hear she got the rash in her nose."

"That kid needs to learn not to put stuff in her nose."

"Appears she hasn't learned that lesson yet. I ran into Doc today, and he said to say hi. He's off oxygen now."

"That's great news. Odd as it may seem, I miss the old duffer and the days when the most serious injury is some hot guy slicing his hand on window flashing."

"What an idiot. Everyone knows window flashing is dangerous," he teased.

"I miss you."

"Miss you, too." He hated this part. The part where all he wanted to do was tell her to get her ass home but couldn't because if she came back to him it had to be her decision.

"How's Sarge?"

"He's back in your bed." The dog slept there all day. "I tried to change the sheets last week and he growled at me."

"I'll have to straighten him out when I come for a visit."

"You're coming for a visit?"

He could almost imagine the smile on her face. "Yes. Can I stay with you?"

"You're not staying with anyone else." Though it had only been weeks, he missed her like it had been years. Long distance wasn't what he wanted, but until Lydia was certain she'd stay in Colorado Springs, he'd take what she could give him. "When are you coming back?"

"I thought Sunday after my shift. I have to be back on Tuesday for a twelve hour."

If she was coming home in three days, he didn't have

much time to get the place ready. "Sunday is great. Should I invite your sister and Cannon over? I can barbecue."

She was silent for a breath. "No. I want you all to myself. We can meet on Monday for dinner if she wants to see me."

"Sunday it is."

The next few days he left the Guild Center and the firehouse to his subcontractors. There was something he wanted to do for Lydia. His house was an accident waiting to happen. With a garden filled with flowers and not a place for her to sit that wasn't exposed, he re-landscaped with evergreens and succulents. While he couldn't produce a bee-free garden, he could reduce the flybys by reducing the flowering buds.

After screening the porch and the pergola, he raced to the shower, hoping he'd timed it all right.

He'd just stepped out of the water when Sarge barked. Wes debated on whether to take a minute to throw clothes on or race to the door in a towel. His childlike excitement had him taking the stairs two at a time and barely getting the towel wrapped around his waist before he flung the door open.

Lydia stood there in jeans and T-shirt. Though she looked tired, he'd never seen her look more beautiful. Just the sight of her made his towel tent. Something she didn't fail to notice.

"Happy to see me?"

He didn't have time to answer because Sarge barreled down the hallway and knocked them both over. Wes had never seen a dog so attention starved. It didn't matter that he'd spent hours giving the mutt love. All Sarge wanted was Lydia. In that way, he and the beast had a lot in common.

"It's nice to be missed." She wiped the dog kisses from

her face. "While I like Sarge's enthusiasm, I'd rather have your kisses." She pushed the dog off and pulled Wes on top of her body.

Sarge skulked into the living room while Wes made love to Lydia on the floor of the entry. With the first round out of the way, he led her to the back porch where he lit candles and poured wine. He covered her naked body with a blanket and they sat together on the settee and watched the sun set.

"You screened the porch?" She nuzzled up against him. He reveled in her presence.

The moment was perfect. He didn't expect to ravish her on the hardwood floor, but any second spent not touching her body was a second wasted.

"I wanted to provide you with a safe place to relax. I screened the pergola too. You once said you'd love to sit out there and read a book. I want you to be able to do that when you visit."

He saw the appreciation in her eyes. As tired as she was, there was a sparkle in them that wasn't there when he answered the door. It made him wish he could put that light in her eyes each day. It wouldn't be a problem if she'd just come home.

"You're too good. I don't deserve you." She never complained about her job or the hours. Not really. Something told him she wanted to, but he knew she thought he'd tell her she'd chosen poorly. He believed that deep in his bones, but he'd never tell her to her face. That decision had to be hers and hers alone. "What if you f-f-find someone else?" She stuttered on the words.

He pulled her into his lap. "I'm not looking for anyone else."

"Not yet but..." She finished her wine and snuggled into

his side. He loved how she felt in his arms. How she smelled and tasted.

"Don't borrow trouble that's not here." They both knew long distance wouldn't work long term, but for now it was fine.

"Thank you for forcing me to go."

He didn't expect that. Was she telling him the choice was a good one? "Are you happy?"

"No, but I'm happy I went. It was something I needed to do. I needed perspective."

Something told him this conversation wasn't going in the direction he hoped. What he wanted was for her to tell him she'd made the wrong choice and fought for the wrong thing.

"It's important to fight for what you want." He knew all too well. He'd given up everything for his dream. If she needed to give him up, he'd understand. It would hurt like hell, but it would be for the best.

"I'm still figuring it out."

"Nothing to figure out tonight except whether you'd like another glass of wine before I take you to bed and ravish you."

She dropped the blanket and raced him for the stairs.

They spent hours in bed loving each other and finally came up for air when their stomachs were louder than their moans of pleasure. They needed nourishment to continue at their pace and food became the new priority. They showered, dressed, and left the house in search of food.

Word got around town she was back for a visit. By dinnertime the diner was full of people wanting to hear about her new life. She visited table after table telling them how busy the city was. How the housing market wasn't good for buyers. How the traffic backed up for miles on the highway. She hated the wait times at restaurants and ate in the cafeteria at work most days. Though she smiled while she spoke, there was no sparkle in her eyes when she talked about the hospital and the people she worked with.

That night he took her home. They sat under the twinkling lights on the pergola. "What's your schedule like this week?" he asked.

"Oh you know, I'm sure I'll see at least two dozen runny noses that were described as life-threatening on the intake form. Someone will cut their finger off with a mower or a weed whacker. There will be an animal bite or two, no doubt several car accidents. If I'm lucky, I'll get to deliver a baby in the hallway. What about you?"

"I've got electrical inspections at the Guild Center this week. If I can squeak in some free time, I need to pick out paint for the house." The paint was still peeling. It was the last thing he needed to do on the exterior to bring it up to date. "What color would you paint it?"

"I know nothing about paint."

"You don't have to know anything. You have to have an opinion."

She thought on it for a minute.

Moths flew into the screen, trying to get to the light. He knew how they felt. Lydia was the light and he was the moth.

"What about butter yellow with cream trim and rust accents?"

He pictured that in his mind. A yellow house with cream colored trim and rust shutters, corbels, and accents. "That would work."

"You're easy."

He pulled the plug on the lights and tossed a few chair

cushions to the floor. His yard was private so there was no real risk of them being seen. "And cheap."

He laid her down on top the cushions, removed her clothing and set out to make love to her in a way she'd remember until the day she died.

He covered her with kisses from her toes to the top of her head. She wiggled and writhed beneath his tongue. The louder she got, the more he gave her. He didn't care if the universe heard her scream his name. In his heart, she belonged to him and that scream proved it. He pulled her to pleasure several times before he sank himself inside her. There was nothing sweeter than when she gave herself to him completely.

He inched himself inside her until their two bodies became one. He pulled and she pushed. He gave and she took. Slowly, he brought her to the peak. He expected her to call out his name like she usually did. But tonight she said, "I love you," and his heart filled with her love.

He wasn't sure of anything but love. There was no guarantee that after tonight she'd ever come back. Part of him wanted to ask her if love would ever be enough, but he was afraid of her answer. Was this trip to Aspen Cove a litmus test? Was it everything she remembered it to be or was it less? He wanted to make sure it was more.

CHAPTER TWENTY-SEVEN

By Wednesday, Lydia was crawling the walls of the ER. Everything irritated the crap out of her from the brightness of the lights to the smell of the wax they used on the floor. Despite the chaos that came with working in emergency medicine, she was bored.

She thought back to the day she removed Wes's stitches. The day he told her about his friend's cancelled trip to Paris.

She wanted to smack herself upside the head. Wes knew if the choice had been hers, she would have found a way to Paris. Hell, she had. She'd gotten to *her* Paris, which was Memorial Hospital. While it was a great place for most people, it wasn't the place for her. It had everything she wanted, and nothing she needed. She worked around the clock and her reward was sore feet and dark circles under her eyes. There were no smiley-face stickers. No tamale pies. No Bailey Brown. Most of all there were no slobbery dog kisses. No Jiffy Pop and scary movies. No yard art hostages. No Wes.

Grandma Dotty always told her to fight for what she wanted. Lydia had fought to get where she was now but surely wants had to come second to needs. The biggest battle to fight and hardest to win was a battle for love. She'd raised the white flag with Adam before the battle had begun because deep down she knew he wasn't a prize worth fighting for. Wes was a different story. He'd thrown up the white flag so she could retreat with honor. Did he somehow know she'd come back to him?

Nothing was certain, but when he made love to her that last night, it wasn't him saying goodbye, but him begging her to stay. She felt the tether of his love with each caress and each kiss. She wanted more. Needed more.

When the head of the department walked in, Lydia asked him for a minute of his time. They retreated to his office, where she thanked him for the opportunity to work there but told him the job wasn't everything she needed it to be.

"Do you know what you're giving up?" he asked.

She smiled. "Yes, but I know it's nothing compared to what I'll gain by leaving."

She finished her shift and went back to the hotel to pack. She had a lot of planning to do. Wes was a romantic. He'd shown her from the twinkling lights on the pergola to the coffee he served her in bed. He never failed to show her how much she mattered. That's all she needed—to matter to someone.

She spent hours writing the reasons she loved Wes on six thousand Post-it Notes. It was what she needed to cover his truck. Go big or go home.

SHE'D PARKED down the street in the dark of the night and snuck back to Wes's house like a thief. Funny how when she'd arrived in Aspen Cove all she thought she needed was a prominent position, a generous paycheck and a caffeine IV drip. She'd never been more wrong. Writing notes with all the ways she loved Wes made her realize there were three things in life she couldn't live without. Wes's kisses, Wes's hugs and Wes's love. Everything else was noise. She pasted the last Post-it on the car. It was a simple smiling face because that's how she felt in his presence.

She stood back and found herself washed in light. As luck would have it, Sheriff Cooper had caught her.

"Are you being bad again?" he asked.

Lydia smiled. "I'm so bad, I'm good."

The sheriff exited his cruiser and walked around the truck. "Does this mean you're back to stay?"

She stepped back and looked at her masterpiece. It had taken four hours to cover every bit of black paint in yellow sticky notes. "I'm back if he'll keep me."

"Are you going to wait until he wakes up to find out?"

"You got another idea?" She hadn't thought past putting the notes on the car. She'd considered a ding-dong ditch where she'd push the doorbell and hide behind a tree.

The sheriff grinned. "I do." He took the handcuffs from his belt and put them on her.

She didn't like the feel of the metal on her wrists. Despite them being loose, they bit into her skin.

Playing her part as the convict, her head hung low as she stood on the front porch while Sheriff Cooper beat on the door. Beneath their feet was a new addition. A smiley-face welcome mat. Looking at it told her she was home.

First to arrive at the door was a barking Sarge. Next came Wes, who opened it looking just-out-of-bed sexy. When he saw Sheriff Cooper his eyes got wide. When he saw Lydia they nearly popped out of his head.

"What the hell?"

"Found her vandalizing your truck."

Wes looked past them to his Post-it Note-covered truck. "Wow!" Barefoot, he walked outside and circled his truck. He plucked note after note. His smile grew with each message.

"You want to press charges?" Sheriff Cooper asked.

Wes brushed his hand over his scruff. "I think there should be some kind of punishment or restitution, don't you?"

Sheriff Cooper led Lydia to Wes. He pulled the cuff key off his ring and handed it to Wes. "I'll leave that up to you. Bring back my cuffs when you're done."

"Hey, wait a minute," Lydia complained. "You can't leave me cuffed."

"I can do what I want, I'm the sheriff. Before you complain, don't forget I'm still picking toilet paper off my trees."

He walked to his squad car and drove away.

Wes continued to pluck yellow notes.

"You love me?" he asked.

"I do."

"What does this mean?" He pointed to his truck.

Lydia moved next to him. "It means I went to Paris and thought it sucked. Paris didn't have you."

"I don't want to be almost enough, Lydia."

"You're more than enough. You're everything I need."

He wrapped his arms around her. "You're just plain

everything." He kissed her long and deep. "Not everything. I want marriage and kids."

"You want a lot." She shook her cuffed wrists. "Uncuff me."

He shook his head. "Not yet." He pulled the notes off his car and read each one.

I love your eyes.

I love your smile.

I love your...

He finished all the ways she loved him and moved on to the promises she made him.

I promise to love you.

I promise to love your dog.

I promise to take my EpiPen everywhere.

I promise to stitch you up.

I promise to never leave you.

I promise my heart belongs to only you.

"How many promises did you make me?"

She shrugged. "At least a hundred. I'll make you a hundred more if you unlock these damn cuffs."

He slid the key into the lock but didn't release her.

"I only need one promise from you." He leaned in and whispered in her ear. "Promise me the second you're loose, you'll be in our bed and naked. I don't have the proper stuff, no ring or pretty words, but when our bodies connect it means forever, sweetheart, so when the cuffs are loose you've got two choices. Turn and leave or promise me forever."

The cuffs fell to the ground and Lydia raced for the door.

She was naked and waiting when Wes arrived. He was as good as his word. He gave her his body and took her heart.

THREE WEEKS LATER, Wes made her his forever. Leave it to a contractor to figure out a way to tent the whole backyard so she didn't get stung. Wes wasn't leaving anything to chance when he stood inside the screened pergola and made her his wife.

Doc was almost finished with their official vows when Wes held up his hand.

"Lydia and I wrote a few things we wanted to add." He held her hands and looked deep into her eyes.

"I promise to be your forever," she began.

"I promise to be your more each day of our lives," Wes said.

"I promise to kiss your boo-boos and heal your wounds and hide any needles."

"I promise to pour your wine, make your coffee, and run your baths."

"I promise to love you more than anything."

Wes gave her a devious smile. "I promise to love you more than chicken wings."

Lydia reached inside his tuxedo and pinched the tiniest bit of skin. When he yelped, Doc said, "I give you Mr. and Mrs. Covington."

Wes and Lydia kissed to the whoops and hollers of the people they now called family.

On the tiny stage in the corner, Samantha sang them a song she'd written called "Passion and Post-it Notes."

"I love you," Wes told her.

"I love you more." Dressed in a simple white gown, Lydia turned her back and tossed her bouquet into the air only to have the spry Agatha Guild catch it.

"Hey, Doc, looks like I'll be calling you Uncle Parker soon." Wes patted the old man on the back.

Doc dismissed him with a wave and walked to the bar.

The men lined up while Wes took a knee and removed the lacy garter from Lydia's thigh. He pulled the elastic back and let it loose into the crowd. The white piece of satin flew straight for Sheriff Cooper. It popped him in the head before falling to the ground. He picked it up and smiled before tucking it inside his pocket.

"You're next, Sheriff," Lydia razzed.

"I'm game if you got the girl."

"I hear there's a new single mother in town. Her name is Marina and she's renting the house next to yours." Marina had brought her adorable daughter in for a checkup, and the second Lydia met her, she knew she'd just met the sheriff's perfect match.

Louise Williams tore the foil from the dishes on the buffet table. She was feeding two for the eighth time. Since her last child was born in the clinic, Lydia hoped the updates her husband planned would be finished by the time the next baby Williams was born, which should be around Christmastime.

As a child she'd dreamed of her wedding day. She wanted lots of flowers, a big church ceremony, and a massive reception with a champagne fountain and a three-tier cake.

In a small town, there was no need for a caterer. Everyone brought a dish to share. There was enough tamale pie to last Lydia a lifetime. A champagne fountain, while nice, didn't beat the bar the Bishops set up along the fence or the alcohol they donated. Knowing the resident baker made getting a wedding cake easy. That it tilted to the right by an inch made it that much sweeter because nothing was perfect in Aspen Cove, but Aspen Cove was the perfect place to live. As she looked around her backyard at the people she'd grown to love, she knew it would always be enough.

OTHER BOOKS BY KELLY COLLINS

An Aspen Cove Romance Series

One Hundred Reasons

One Hundred Heartbeats

One Hundred Wishes

One Hundred Promises

One Hundred Excuses

One Hundred Christmas Kisses

One Hundred Lifetimes

One Hundred Ways

One Hundred Goodbyes

One Hundred Secrets

One Hundred Regrets

One Hundred Choices

One Hundred Decisions

One Hundred Glances

One Hundred Lessons

One Hundred Mistakes

One Hundred Nights

One Hundred Whispers

One Hundred Reflections

One Hundred Intentions

One Hundred Chances

One Hundred Dreams

GET A FREE BOOK.

Go to www.authorkellycollins.com

ABOUT THE AUTHOR

International bestselling author of more than thirty novels, Kelly Collins writes with the intention of keeping love alive. Always a romantic, she blends real-life events with her vivid imagination to create characters and stories that lovers of contemporary romance, new adult, and romantic suspense will return to again and again.

For More Information
www.authorkellycollins.com
kelly@authorkellycollins.com

Printed in Great Britain
by Amazon

33856294R00129